D0953771

CHIMPANZEE

Also by Darin Bradley

Noise

CHIMPANZEE

DARIN BRADLEY

Underland Press

This is U014, and it has an ISBN of 978-1-63023-000-5.

This book was printed in the United States of America, and it is published by Underland Press, an imprint of Resurrection House (Puyallup, WA).

Do not run in straight lines.

Edited by Mark Teppo
Cover Design by Jennifer Tough
Book Design by Aaron Leis
Copy Edit by Shannon Page

First Hardback Underland Press Edition: September 2014.

www.resurrectionhouse.com

For Rima

CHAPTER ONE

THEY DIDN'T ALWAYS SHOOT PEOPLE.

In the beginning, when civic offenders were conscripted into the Homeland Renewal Project, they were monitored only by crew chiefs. Hourly employees with managerial experience. People used time sheets. Signatures. They carried their meals with them in paper bags.

But when the crews organized, when they started collecting protection money, to keep you from harm at the hands of other people on the crew—gang affiliations, race riots—workers disappeared. The crews became micro-politics. They followed the examples of the mobs in the larger cities, looking for someone to blame. They carried weapons in their lunch bags. Renewal became a safe opportunity to sell your contraband, in your standard-issue, reflective red jumpsuit.

They deputized the crew chiefs. Gave them shotguns. At first, they tried non-lethal rounds, but those caused an uprising. So they killed a few. It no longer makes the news.

○

The lien against my education is twenty-three pages long. It contains abbreviated transcripts of my yearly audits, when I, like every other student borrower, sat down in the loan therapist's office on campus and let him index my cognitive chemical tendencies, my entrained associations, my affective self-models, which source most of my intellect.

It's important to remember that we are not "in charge." You don't own your body, it owns you. It's the same thing.

You don't own your education. It's on loan until you pay it off.

○

I am good at being unemployed. I can act interested and positive when Sireen, my wife, calls to check on me in the middle of the day. She stays concerned about my moods. About all of this.

I am good at walking downtown—from our borough at the other end of the city because Sireen and I lease only one car, which she needs for the job she still has. I know which blocks are the most vacant, so to avoid them. I know whom to talk to. I know which times of day are safe for spending an hour in Sentinel Park, in the heart of downtown, doing nothing but being a guy with a coffee sitting in a park.

○

It's an illusion, Sireen said. She was irritated. The wind kept blowing her hair against her mouth while she tried to eat. It was a bad day to wear it down.

Sleight-of-hand, she said. But I had told her I liked it down. It's how I knew this was working.

Each year of my education—each year of new cognitive associations—expanded the previous year's index. Because association doesn't mean causation.

Just because two variables are correlated doesn't mean they caused each other, she said. She put her sandwich in her lap to do something about this. Nothing was growing in the flowerbeds behind us, and their bricks were cold.

If it did, that first audit would have always been enough. But subsequent audits charted all the discrete change—chemically and behaviorally.

2

Cum hoc ergo propter hoc, I said.

What? She looked at me with a bad taste in her mouth. Hair.

With this, therefore because of this, I said.

Yes, she said. Obviously. In exchange, she had told me she liked that—how I made things more complicated. It made her laugh.

It's a logical fallacy, I said.

No, she said. We're talking about numbers.

They could detail how I learned. How I connected different principles and theories. How I thought.

Ex nihilo nihil fit.

Teeth in even rows, bleached by the air and sun. Her perpetual smile. It was bright here, on my side of campus. There weren't as many trees.

Learning new conceptual associations pushed causation further away. Every year, the more you learned. At a point, there would be no such thing as ultimate causality. No one to blame for rainbows or bankruptcy or the creation of the universe.

Stop it, she said. I'm eating.

Stop what?

Being you!

○

Eventually, time became money, and no one had any. Least of all the government.

Experts joined the Senate Efficiency Committee to ensure that state agencies were maximizing employee potential. They started doling out tasks randomly in the Homeland Renewal Project. Some days, it's raking gravel at highway construction sites. Other days it's changing bed pans in veterans' hospitals. It's fair, and after they started randomizing the crews every morning, the power organizations of the old crews fell apart.

Incorporating monitors into the project only made sense. As monitors, Renewal workers are given a reprieve from their uniforms and sent out as employees, patients, students—anything that pertains to anything. They report waste or malfeasance.

They expanded into the neighborhoods, and now they have quotas. Failure to produce enough efficiency observations results in extra work hours. Since the monitor program started, no one knows anyone anymore.

The Efficiency Committee became concerned with activities that could foment unrest. The country was no longer a powder keg, but it had dry rot. Anything that could incite anything was considered civic unrest. In some states, that meant fucking the wrong sex. In others, it was reading the wrong books, or jostling the American Dream. Mostly, the Committee doesn't do anything with this information, but monitors collect it.

Sometimes it gets leaked to gangs or cartels or separatists. The ones the Committee finds useful, who'll do something about something.

It's important that Renewal dispatchers randomize their monitors. Different people see different things. Some see inequality. Some see waste. Some don't see anything at all. They're all the same, and it's all about perceptual readiness and environmental priming.

I should know. I studied all of this in graduate school. Perception isn't about receiving information. It's about creating it. The world in your own image.

○

The yearly audits are important because educations are not repossessed wholesale—repossession therapists go after aspects of your education one at a time, starting with the most recent, in the hopes that you'll get a job and start repaying the loans before they have to repossess your entire education, which is your means of earning to pay anything back.

With everyone gone bankrupt, though, it no longer matters. There aren't many still borrowing their ways through college.

After 365 consistent days without a job, I have exceeded the allowable forbearance on my student loans. I cannot afford to make payments, even income-adjusted, which requires only partial Renewal service. Sireen and I want to buy a house. Start a family. So, we have options. We can empty our meager savings to buy another few months with my degrees, so I can pursue jobs that don't exist, to provide for a wife and a *someday* child that don't need me to. Sireen's income covers our rent, which the university adjusted for us as a courtesy, after my dismissal, because, among many, they own the house we rent. Her income covers our car payment, our utilities, the credit cards we keep at a modest balance to maintain her rating. She feeds us.

I have the option to make direct payments to the loans that financed my Master's degree, my Bachelor's, so I can keep them longer while they go after my Ph.D. So I might manage a decent conversation with Sireen at our dinner table, over inexpensive wine and discounted, factory-produced meats. We could use these degrees to spend more time *thinking* about a family. We might watch more programs about birth. About home renovation and investment. Getting ready. We might age Biblically, into our hundreds. We might sleep in caves for generations and emerge after the flood, to start our lives then. I could give Sireen a child in another life, still educated enough in this one to know such places exist.

But I cannot get the teaching jobs that don't exist at the universities that aren't hiring without my Ph.D. They're a package deal, those degrees. We must devour them all, like defective young or upstart gods. Like flesh. A Eucharist become our domestic dream, our shared lives. People have been creating things by consumption for a long time. Monsters. Men. Personal saviors and vision guides. It's nothing out of the ordinary.

Three different degrees in literature and literary theory. So I can know things like that. I specialized in cognitive theory and how it informs abstract fiction.

○

After ninety days, if I do not report for repossession therapy, if I do not enlist in Homeland Renewal, then municipal officers will issue warrants for my arrest. They will initiate repossession therapy anyway. They will assign me to a Renewal dispatcher, and they will begin garnishing my payments from Sireen's paycheck.

While I work Renewal, I will be fed two state meals during my shifts because no one is allowed to bring anything along anymore. No paper bags.

The same thing happens if you fail to pay your parking tickets, or file your taxes. Child support. They're acts of civic fraud, which are categorized as domestic terrorism against the common good. Not everyone has an education to surrender—those people work longer sentences.

In my case, it's reneging on my financial agreements with the Department of Education. It's theft, and it must be deterred—repossession alone is insufficient. Other borrowers need to be scared away from actions like mine. As if most of us have any kind of choice. As if we've got better things to do with the money we don't have than pay our debts.

Sireen teaches math at Central University, where I worked, and we make her loan payments on time. Because we must. After we graduated, she found a job first, a permanent one, and I followed her. That was our deal.

I did what I could.

○

My Renewal dispatcher works in a construction trailer in a municipal parking lot downtown, behind the main post office. There are no cars in the spaces. There are weeds between veins of exposed tar. An a/c window-unit sweats beside the front door, making puddles on the concrete for algae and other green things.

Men and women, in their vivid Renewal jumpsuits, stand around. A few wear plain clothes. Most of them are black or Hispanic. You ring the buzzer to get into the trailer—a red utility light beside the door lights up when you may enter. Like a therapist's office. Or a sound stage.

Inside the trailer, a black man with a salt-and-pepper beard sits at an aluminum desk. His eyes glow behind a computer screen, which shines on photographs of children. They face me—on display. He can't see them from where he sits. His nameplate reads JEREMIAH ROSEMEADE.

He looks up, back down. "Name?"

"Benjamin Cade," I say.

There are red jumpsuits on hangers against the far wall.

He glances at the suits, too.

"Go pick one out. They're sorted by height."

It feels like a PVC tarp, with sleeves and cuffs. The lapels can be lifted and zipped around the nose and mouth.

"Three years," he says.

"Right," I say.

"Mandatory repossession therapy." He looks at me. "Professor."

Not that I ever was. That would connote permanence. A job for the ages. But whatever.

His printer ejects a slip of paper, and he offers it around the computer screen. The linoleum squeaks as I cross the room back to his desk.

"Your therapist is Cynthia St. Claire. Her office is at 520 North Main, Suite 3. You will report to her within five days."

"Yes, sir," I say.

He stops and looks at me. "I'm Rosie," he says.

I wonder what bills he pays. How he earned his way up to this job. There is a shotgun leaning against a windowless door behind his desk.

He goes back to his screen. "You'll report here by 6:00 AM, every shift. Meals will be provided. Wear comfortable shoes."

I act attentive. Like I did at orientation, at each of the schools that have employed me. The same spiel every time, to make you feel welcome.

"Do I really need to go over everything?" Rosie says.

"No, sir."

"There's some literature in that cubby. Feel free."

"Yes, sir."

He untangles a thumbprint scanner from the cables on his desk. Offers it up in his hand, like some palmist's secret.

"Give me your print," he says.

I think about words unto flesh. The mark of the beast. But it's just a scanner. This is just a trailer. Rosie is just another man.

I give him my print.

When Sireen calls me, here, downtown, I step into the alcove of what was once the indie-theater's canopied entrance. It was still open when we moved into town. Sometimes, on Sunday afternoons, Sireen and I would come for a movie. We'd take turns: she always picked French films—things full of space and contrast and meaningful settings. She learned it growing up, with English and Arabic, so she would listen—placing herself in conversations I couldn't follow. I would watch her instead—the projector light on the slicks of her eyes—and listen to them babble. When it was my turn, I would pick existential dramas about nothing, which I convinced myself I liked. Sireen would hold my hand, as if we were watching horror films.

The sun is out today, so the people are too. Loitering. Exchanging stories. Taking up space. I don't want to be in anybody's way while I talk.

"Hey," I say.

"Hey," Sireen says. It's quiet around her. "What's up downtown? Did you make your appointment?"

I don't respond to the first question, which is all right.

"On my way."

"Did you get some lunch?"

I was too nervous to eat.

"Yeah."

I stand in the alcove, waiting out the silence of what to say next, which is the most important part of these phone calls.

"Are you all right?" she says.

"Yeah."

"Sure?"

"Yeah."

"Do you want to go to dinner tonight?" she says.

No.

"Sure."

"Dimitri and I agreed to take one of the candidates out to his dinner. I think you ought to come."

Her department is hiring. A campus visit, the necessary pilgrimage, is part of every academic's job search. Usually, a department hosts a few of them—one per candidate. The dinner is one of the most important parts. When the candidate is told to relax and not to worry about his or her performance of self. Which is not the truth. Other faculty, from other departments, are usually in the mix, like Dimitri, who is not in Sireen's department. He is a sociologist. Inviting faculty from other departments demonstrates academic diversity.

"Okay," I say.

"Could you shave?"

"What?"

"Well, I just want . . . I don't want to make the wrong impression, you know? Until tenure."

"I can grow my beard when you get tenure?"

"Ben, come on," she says. "It just . . . you could just trim it."

"Yeah."

"Yeah, what?"

"I said 'yeah.'"

○

Repossession is therapeutic, the promissory note to my student loans explains. Painless. Repossessing aspects of associative thought, of "cerebro-ontogenetic development," will, at worst, result in disorientation and nausea. Other side effects occur in rare instances.

They can't take the data out of your head. That's impossible. They just make it something traumatic. Something to squirrel away in the small dark of your lower consciousness, where it becomes nightmares and suppressed experiences and terrible memories. The brain does the work for them by protecting itself from what's become unpleasant. It's like forgetting. Eating the lotus.

You can't use what's theirs if you can't pay for it, which makes sense. They financed it, after all. Collegiate enrollment spiked after everyone discovered that they were under-degreed to compete for dwindling employment, and several senators won their offices by campaigning for college degrees for everyone. But educating everyone doesn't necessarily make them any money. Academic accreditation boards put caps on the number of graduates a university could produce in a given year. Because degrees had become so common, so easy to get, they no longer differentiated anyone in the workforce. The Department of Education had no choice but to start using our indices, from our audits. They were maps to a better future.

Educating everyone doesn't make the workforce any money, but repossessing degrees makes it for the banks. The moneylenders whose investments in an educated America are underwritten by the government itself. Reclaiming possession of a borrower's indices is good for research, and it improves the fiscal odds for those graduates who can still make money by increasing the rarity and value of their degrees—those still capable of making their loan payments. The hope is that these achievers will create our new generation of jobs, above and beyond the corporate ladder, and we can all start again next time. With a new generation.

It's for the greater good.

○

Downtown, I find my loan therapist's office. The oxidized brass door handles. The nondescript text on the office door. REPOSSESSION THERAPY in clean Helvetica font. My phone vibrates, so I pull it out of my pocket before going in.

It's a text message from Sireen.

Sorry about the beard ;)

CHAPTER TWO

BEHIND ALL THIS, THE NEW DEPRESSION, THE MEANS OF production are fine. They were never the problem. Of course the workers went on strike. Of course there were Kangaroo Negotiations. Of course tear gas, and arson, and that perpetual image: young men throwing stones—a Biblical act, an assertion of lineage, of community. Justice. They threw them because they could. Because someone had to. Never mind the union men. This was talismanic. A sacred rite passed from fathers to sons.

The *means* of production were never the problem. They were the question, begging itself. It's the *production* that needs revolution. There are no means to an end.

I used to teach my students not to beg the question.

In the end, the ousted workers were invited to produce whatever they damn well pleased with the machinery. With the line assemblies. With the break rooms and warehouses. Because it didn't matter. No one was buying anything, so there was no producing.

Of course there were strikes. By that point, there were so many workers gone, so many forming lines, echelons, phalanxes on the concrete fields behind the picket line. It wasn't even mob mentality. It was herd. Gathering in numbers against the inevitable. The country demonstrated and protested, full of sound and fury, until, eventually, we just didn't anymore. We were exhausted and hungry. And still unemployed. The only way to eat was to get in line and shut up. The government was sorry about all this—it really was. They all were.

Had we really cared, we would have simply burned everything. The factories, the offices, the servers and routers. Everything.

✧

In therapists' offices, like this one, a hand always comes first, dowsing through the just-open door while the therapist conveys whatever *very-necessary*, last-minute instructions on the other side—to the receptionist, or the insurance rep, or the previous client, who won't stop having issues even as he's signing papers at the front desk.

This is called "priming," and it sources a particular subject role for the therapist. It's nothing strange. Consciousness takes form in the situation around it. Identity is context. I tried to explain it to Sireen, over beers one afternoon in the bar at the edge of campus. We were with her math friends, and they laughed and called me a nihilist. Liberal arts. Sireen laughed, too. I realized then that it was funny, and she laid her fingers across the back of my hand. We weren't married yet, and I was trying too hard.

So, I sourced a new me that day. I remember. One amused by myself. Later, drunk, we lay on the flattened carpet in her tiny living room, smoking and listening to obscure bands I pretended to know.

> Someone was singing in Norwegian. I kissed her, and she tasted like apple vodka. We slept there, under some aunt's afghan, and Sireen muttered vowels at her dreams.

I am both subject and object in this office because that's how this works. I have been primed to recognize time limits (55 minutes), authority (the therapist), and slight sexual arousal (manicured fingers and a panty-hosed kneecap).

We could also call this a "hook." It defines and sustains my interest in this encounter. Everything begins by making your audience pay attention.

"Dr. Cade?" the therapist says, her hand once more leading the way as she commits to entering the office for good. She extends it to shake.

This is the same gesture we use to keep assailants at bay. But then, she would be more object than subject. A victim-to-be.

"Yes," I say.

"I'm Cynthia."

She wears her hair down. Which helps.

"Can I get you anything?" she says. "Are you comfortable?"

"No."

That stops her just enough. She should know better, cramming those two questions together.

When she sits down, she is careful to tug her skirt toward her knees.

"First of all," she makes eye contact—a professional, "thank you for coming."

I smile. "Of course."

"Have you read the introductory literature?"

"Yes."

"Can I call you 'Benjamin?'"

"You may."

"Well, Benjamin, today we won't begin therapy. This is a chance to get to know each other."

I want to say this is *my* chance. She'll have to get to know me all over again. Each time, as there is less of me to know. Blocking my education is going to take a few memories with it. Situations and contexts and exactly what it was like to learn this, or this, or this thing. Did a theory click for me in the shower, on a walk, during sex? It will take with it anything that pertains. My life, on borrowed time.

"Let's begin with questions," she says. "What can I tell you? About our office? The process? Me?"

"Let's talk about value," I say.

"I'm sorry?"

"Let's discuss how repossessing my education recovers the government's lost investment."

"Benjamin, the investment isn't lost yet."

"Ben."

"Fine, Ben."

She looks at her file, on her computer pad, which rests like a clipboard on her knees. Her skirt has receded, slowly, and now it's several inches up her thighs.

These are things I shouldn't notice. But I do. I try to think about Sireen.

"Your father suffered from frontotemporal dementia," she says. Looks at me.

"I don't want to talk about my father."

"Working through longitudinal analyses of progressive indices, like yours, is making great strides in experimental treatments for dementia sufferers," she says. "Like your father."

I don't say anything. My mom cried when I told her about repossession. She just kept apologizing. Thanking God Dad wasn't around for it. He didn't think it was a good idea. The debt. The degrees. The idle study—the hours in libraries. He liked me just the way I was. Used to say it, when he was lucid. *Just the way you are, son.* Stuck in a timewarp. Warning me against myself over and over like some sentimental fugue.

"Why don't we change the subject," Cynthia says. She makes eye contact again. "Your dissertation was about cognitive theory. Tell me how to define a 'self.'"

○

By the end of my last semester, before my appointment expired at our university, I just gave all my students "A"s. Because they weren't the point. They were just a necessity, and I needed all the time I could get, which I mostly spent sitting on our front porch, drinking beer and twisting shoots off of Sireen's morning glories. I couldn't tell if I was feeling sorry for myself or making big plans. Nothing came together, either way.

Sireen and I were lucky. Our university was private, which meant that it lost funding immediately—straight from the endowment, when the stock markets started sliding. So we knew. The administration knew what to do immediately. Whose contracts they couldn't renew.

The public universities went later, in size, in number. Surprised when their states started choking off cash flows. Property tax funds fell when foreclosures rose, when commercial buildings went vacant and office parks in-progress slipped into half-constructed limbo. Jobs followed. Income and sales went with them. Taxes became what we wished we could pay. We didn't need representation anymore—we needed fucking taxation.

Many of the public universities were dissolved, along with some municipal services. Tuition climbed to cover budget gaps. Most smaller schools folded, sacrifices to the larger, who trucked in temporary buildings and festival-sized tents to accommodate all the new enrollees. It was an Age of Enlightenment. Education would be the answer, from the top down.

Faculty were released. Temporary, or part-time, mostly. Like me. Full-time faculty absorbed our teaching loads, creating classes so massive that the students had to teach themselves, largely through support groups and banks of communal notes. The faculty left behind their specializations and started teaching introduction to composition, and introduction to philosophy, and introduction to world religions. College algebra. Macroeconomics. Political Science. The new university is mostly introductory, and no one cares who will pick up the task of advancing this basic knowledge.

It was decided that departments would offer fewer upper-level courses within a given major, less often. It now takes the students longer, costs them more, and leaves them with dangerous ideas—the ideas of ideas—about disciplines that do more harm than good when left without conclusions.

When we were children, we did not play with fire, but we loved the smell of gasoline. Someone was around to teach us the advanced consequences of studying combustion.

○

This is not unusual. People often fill Sentinel Park. For drum circles. Footbag. Outdoor chess. Sometimes, on Saturdays, the city hosts children's contests. Hula Hoop tournaments, or dance-offs, or synchronized jump-rope. It's a reason to come downtown—other than bread lines and employment offices. A way to be a family. The idea is to stimulate the local economy. After dark, though, most people don't come here because there are always too many transients, staying out of trouble in one place.

It isn't much of a park. It's an amphitheater, really—slabs of cement shelving down into the earth, twenty feet or so beneath

15

street level. There is no green space—the park is an urban hollow, a leftover gap between three streets converging in the old retail district. There is a gazebo on one side, a wrought-iron, powder-coated thing. Open-air, because that's nice.

The speaker, in that gazebo, doesn't need a megaphone. I can't tell exactly how many people have crowded themselves into the bottom-level flatspace to listen. From this angle, walking back toward my borough, I can only see the crowd's marbled heads, swaying.

We have class division again. University students are rich; their parents are rich—they have to be. The students take courses in poverty studies. They take part in poverty tours and poverty simulations. Financial aid is no longer a solvent investment, and it will disappear soon. It will follow the banks under the national umbrella, to reappear as highway construction and parks renovation. Anything that will create work.

Among other things.

The speaker in the gazebo has a posse—four or five comrades standing, staring, or lending their ears. They're all wearing rubber chimpanzee masks.

"Don't 'buy local'," he shouts. "Don't buy *anything at all.*"

I look around. This is something. It takes courage, because they'll be arrested. I'm surprised they were even able to gather for this long. Someone had to orchestrate it—get the word out. Crowds attract attention—they force outsiders to exist with the protest or performance or whatever. A network of brains, making the thing real for just however long.

Which would be what these chimpanzee kids were after. Sucking your awareness in, just long enough. Making the audience pay attention.

"Don't *organize*," the speaker shouts. "You can't sustain yourselves. Not without food. Without funding. Without a workforce subor-dinate to your will."

I duck out of the sidewalk traffic to turn my phone back on. It vibrates—another message from Sireen.

Dinner canceled. Candidate already took competing offer. Not coming.

"You don't have any idea what *money* even *is*," the speaker shouts. "It's just a token. It's a convenient way to carry what, in theory, you've acquired. Food, water, precious metals. Things other people *want*."

I text her back. Can I buy some beer then?

"And if value is based on scarcity," he shouts, "we're talking about conflict. *Conflict* is value."

People walk past me. They don't look like conflict, laying one footstep after another on the sunblasted concrete. Trying not to make a scene—not to be a part of one.

I feel like I should tell this kid that he's getting his rhetoric wrong. He's got hooks down, but if he turned in this transcript, as a paper, I'd fail him.

Conflict follows value follows organization follows capital exchange. *Non sequitur.* He's putting the cart before the revolutionary horse. He needs to cite some sources—something his crowd can relate to. Quickly, before some Renewal monitor's text messages get to the police and the beatings and chemical dispersant begin.

The phone vibrates again. Babe, stop asking permission.

But the speaker's got something going on. One of his comrades watches him carefully. A girl wearing sexual tension like a too-hot overcoat. This is politics, a bigger something than whatever, so she needs to be damn sure she's read enough, seen enough, demonstrated enough before this entire operation, all this shouting, becomes just a metaphor. An expression between them for what goes on beneath bed sheets on futons in apartments without fixtures over the light bulbs. This "cause"—whatever they're doing, shouting about—is the sex between them *now*, and it will be later, too, when it is nothing more than the parameters of their relationship.

When Sireen and I dated, we talked about critical theory or non-positively curved geometry, which is her field.

> Tell me something, she said. About literature.
>
> About *literature*? I said.
>
> She laughed. That smile lipping morning teeth over her uneven kitchen table. She had found both chairs independently and then painted them, so it was artistic that they didn't match the table. There weren't

any curtains, which just made the nook brighter—
stamped it as hers, where things like light revealed the
unwashed buff of wakeup skin. Where dark things
became darker. Like coffee.

I gave her Derrida, Saussure, De Man. And she traded the
Hausdorff dimension and outer automorphism and lattice-
ordered groups. Mathematics.

Yeah, she said. Come on! I want to think like you do.
She brought her lips together. It deepened the
after-giggle. She did that often—prompting what she
wanted with that female sound. Sourcing things.
Okay, I said, okay. Um, how about border studies.
Trans-regional discourse.
Excited. Yes!

Post-colonialism became a sexual politic. Nil radicals attracted
us. Cognitive theory had no place in Utopian studies, or New
Historicism, and the Moussong metric (on the Davis complex)
meant, well . . . nothing. To me. Graduate school became nothing
between us, which was the point.

Close your eyes.
Closed. Rolling beneath taut-thin lids. Following the
light through the darkness.
Place your fingers on your temples.
Placed. What is this? she said.
Culture. Be quiet. Say om.
Om.
Say oma.
Oma.
Omatul.
Omatul.
Om. Ah. Tul.
Om. Ah. Tul.
Om. Ah. Tul—I'm a tool.
She opened her mouth like her eyes. An unveiling.

Humorshock. She screamed as she laughslapped me.
It actually hurt.

You shit! You shit!

Omatul . . .

I was just talking, looking for ways to keep her smiling. Because I wasn't good at telling dirty jokes, which is mostly what she laughed at. How the guys in her program made her laugh. They watched her move as closely as I did.

○

The crowd likes what the kid had to say. They're all shouting now. Over and around each other. Attracting attention. Being disturbingly obvious.

There are a few more Renewal workers around now. Paying attention. The day laborers, at the other end of the park, who didn't make it quickly enough into the bed of some hiring asshole's pickup truck that morning, are paying attention.

The noise is indecipherable, like nonsense. Or glossolalia—the holy spirit on the move downtown.

I text Sireen back. Okay.

She earns our money, so I ask.

CHAPTER THREE

OUR BAR HAS JUMPED IN ON SOME NEW FAD, SOME GAME, and Dimitri has convinced me to try it. He even set up my login ID and filled in the information for my public profile. We spend plenty of time playing video games at home, during the summers when he and Sireen have time off. She usually just watches us, taking notes sometimes. Compiling them in lists on her computer. Dimitri and I are particularly good at sharing games intended for only one player. Sireen sometimes writes small programs of her own. Things to help her manage all those numbers.

"It's fun," Dimitri says. He smiles as he walks back across the bar.

It begins by not watching the drinks.

I have a beer in each hand, and I have exhausted the game's "free inspection"—already I can't recall tiny details like the printed monogram on the pint glasses. This program simulates obsessive-compulsive disorder—Dimitri selected it from the menu of available disorders to simulate. The goggles I'm wearing are not rigged for VR—I can still see through them, albeit tintedly. There are electrode-pads affixed to my temples and forehead with disposable, sanitary adhesion pads. There are tiny earphones.

The bartender is letting me try this for free. She's just introduced it here. Another way to bring people in. Something else to do. Soon, she will charge per minute.

You get a free inspection of the details around you before the simulation starts—later inspections will "cost" you. The OCD sim is about resisting impulse, resisting inspections. Carrying overfull pints of beer without watching them (to make sure they don't spill) fits the rules.

The carpet here is long and red, faux-Victorian—fleur-de-lis, paisleys, clumps of dotted vines. It's sarcastic. Out of place in the décor of this bar. It's hip.

Through the goggles, through the electrode pulses stimulating artificial neuro-chemical exchange, the carpet is no longer normal. It . . . *spins*, without moving. In asymptotic arcs and Fibonacci spirals. Pressure is gathering at the base of my skull as I study the carpet. Nothing would be finer. Nothing sweeter. Nothing would be more high than inspecting that carpet, tracing, tracing. Walking without stepping on paisleys so I don't break my mother's back. Which is another impulse I must resist.

I can feel the importance, now. I must be sure. I have already inspected the layout of the tables. I will not step on the paisleys. But I will inspect again. I have just inspected, and I do not want to inspect again. I'm starting to feel ashamed. But I will inspect.

Personally, Dimitri told me, he prefers the paranoid schizo sim.

I am afraid to move. I will spill the beer. I must move, though— I'm growing nauseated. My blood is beginning to buzz. The lure of the carpet increases exponentially. I'm not gaining anything by looking at it—I'm losing.

But pushing the episode.

But the thrill.

I look away before I start counting things, like people or dots, which I feel compelled to do. I wish I could stop inspecting. I won't tell anyone how many times I have inspected. I am finished inspecting, so I will just inspect once more.

The beer sloshes when I move. Most likely, this is because of the strange cocktail in my brain, which is guided by low-voltage pulses from the electrodes. Which is disturbing the information in my inner ear. It bends gravity. Spacetime. The physics of simulating someone else's neurological imbalance.

All I have to do is carry the beer to our booth, where Dimitri is sitting, watching, and I'll "win." I'm starting to feel feverish. Acid pumps are spraying my internal organs. Stop inspecting stop inspecting stop inspecting. The burn is crawling up my esophagus. The carpet surges, lapping at table legs and sandaled feet as if swallowing. But it hasn't moved. I can't see where I'm stepping now, which has caused my eyes to begin watering, and the beer is running across my fingers in scalding runnels.

I need to think.

Being. Existing. Me. Controlling this fucking situation is just a complication of "paying attention," which is all awareness is. The goggles are fucking with what I see. I know what they're doing. It's change blindness—they can alter my visual field during the micro-second, saccadic shifts of my eyes. You can make anyone see anything, if you're fast enough, and attention isn't as fast as the microprocessors in these goggles.

But, fuck.

I take a few more steps across the faux-Victorian sea. It used to be carpet.

I need to inspect. I need to inspect. I need to inspect.

I need to think.

It's not real. I can make it. I don't *see* anything. I'm not seeing any of this bullshit. I'm layering proto-objects from low-level neural processing and binding them with the neural excitation of paying attention. I see what I'm paying attention to. Except, in this case, it's what the simulation is paying attention to.

Pay attention pay attention pay attention.

I'm creating scenery. Manipulating what I can recognize from the stupid part of my brain. The kindergarten brain that sees colors and square blocks and knows when it's about to get hit.

Perception is creation. My own fucked-up world.

I'm creating vomit sliding up, up, up. The pressure has increased behind my eyes. I feel the beer falling in slops. I am not supposed to spill the beer.

The goggles make you fuck yourself. A negative affirmation of how you'd like the world to go. They're knock-offs of the equipment that therapists like Cynthia use. My graduate studies director used similar devices in the early days. When he and his gang were figuring it all out.

This isn't fucking fair.

I put another foot forward. I've stepped on a paisley—I can feel it. The muscles clutching my femur shudder, and my groin begins to ache. Have I pissed myself?

Here, here, here, here . . .

There are thirty-three paisleys between me and Dimitri. This is not a prime number. I can step, longly, and not hit any more of them. I need to be sure.

I need to be sure.

Dimitri is suddenly before me. He slips the goggles off my forehead. Yanks the electrode-pads from my skin.

"Jesus," he says.

He gets an arm around me before the sudden-relief vertigo G-forces my eyes closed. Sends me to the floor.

○

He's already bought me four beers, sheepishly. It was supposed to be fun. My head doesn't hurt anymore, so it's all right.

"Well, why is it called 'chimping?'" I say.

Dimitri takes a drag from his cigarette. He watches twenty-somethings in second-hand T-shirts walking in and out of the bar.

"I don't know," he says. "Monkey see, monkey do?"

"I saw chimpanzee masks—at a protest downtown."

He shrugs at me.

I take a drink with a trembling hand.

"You can become addicted to it," he says.

"What?"

"Chimping."

"What do you mean, 'addicted' Like, you want to play it all the time?"

He shrugs again, smokes. "I don't know. I've just heard. Some get stuck on the goggles. Can't function without them. Over time."

"They . . . *live* the simulation? All-the-time goggle-insanity?"

"So I hear."

Dimitri thinks just about everything is "cute," or "asinine," or "telling." He tries most things: new games, drinks. He regularly attends shows at half a dozen venues across town—that is to say, at houses packed with young roommates, overfull with heat and alcohol and insufficient bedspace. They produce "shows" in their living rooms—he can name most of the bands they play in this bar. I can't name any, but it's close to my house, so I can walk here. Dimitri has to walk further. There are usually people along his way, asking for beer or food, and he gives them cash. Sometimes. They would've mugged him already, but he's fast. I only have to walk through my neighborhood.

"Smoke?" he says.

I take one. He gives them to me all the time, now that Sireen and I agreed we shouldn't spend on them. I know he feels sorry for me, but I don't care. I didn't want to quit. And when we started all this, being together, young men full of brains and anger and important opinions. Debating things, shouting things, affirming our shared, bar-time ennui, I still had a job. I still bought my own cigarettes. Expensive drinks. We built ourselves on this, and Dimitri keeps it up. He's my only friend.

One of the bartenders brings two bourbons to the table. She smiles, walks back, and says bartender things to some new-entries. To people who know her name. It is a very particular presentation of self, and not everyone can pull it off.

"I took the liberty," Dimitri says, reaching for a glass.

This isn't unusual, except he ordered the good one. The bourbon we don't order unless we're really just in the mood. We haven't had it since I was able to buy it myself.

"What's the occasion?" I say.

He purses his lips against the liquor. "Tell me about the shrink first."

"She's hot."

"Yeah?"

"Don't start."

He lifts his hands, innocent. Smiling into the smoke between us. He's a sociologist. Studies micro-economies and the politics of exchange. He wrote a paper on what we give up to attractive people.

He drops the smile into his bourbon, like you're supposed to when readying for a topic like this. He projects a new self, sources a new discourse position. An appropriate one.

Although, really, the position sources *him*.

He's ready, I'm ready. That's how it goes.

"How was the session?" he says.

"Fantastic."

"I'm sorry," he says. He makes eye contact. A professional himself. "I didn't mean—"

"It was fine."

A pair of women are chimping at the bar, making out while their friends giggle. Girls' night out. There's a sign behind the bar—five minutes free when you order whatever special. I can't read that part. They're wearing sunglasses, the watching ones.

"Good," he says.

○

Before we came to this town, Sireen and I, Dimitri was alone here. For a while, when I worked with them at the university, it was really something. The three of us carpooled. We listened to public radio, or checked out whatever latest CD he'd picked up from whatever latest DIY house-show. Record store. Whatever.

Before we arrived, he was going to leave town. Get back on the job market and live somewhere else alone. Try again. He would live as his own source of attraction, like a gravity well. He cannot return to his native country because he dodged his mandatory military service to earn his Ph.D. in the U.S. His voice lilts because of his accent—too-perfect consonants like chipping teeth—and he remembers things like food shortages, unstable govern-ments, and grocery stores filled with only one kind of each thing. Communist-issue.

So, having a few years of grad school repossessed, without a job, is not to him what it is to me. We've talked about this.

○

"Do you want to talk about it?" he says.

He and Sireen still carpool.

"She asked about my dissertation."

"Has she read it?"

"Seems like."

"And?"

That last semester, when I gave them all "A"s, now and then, one would ask the right questions, and I could give the answers I wanted. About selfhood and cognition and not being in charge. There were no ghosts in the machine. Now and then, I could undo everything Descartes fucked us with. Because, he had it backwards.

I am; therefore, I think.

I could help them understand being. All the sturm and drang. Even if we were supposed to be talking about writing. It changed a few lives. Mine, I think. Sometimes.

I laugh at Dimitri. "Why are we drinking the good stuff?"

"Tell me more about the shrink."

"She gets it," I say. "I haven't had *that* chance before. I haven't talked, like that, about it. Nobody's followed my theories all the way down the rabbit hole."

"That's ironic."

"I know."

But mostly, I gave them "A"s because they were never supposed to be the point. My education was for *me*. This was my enlightenment, my debt. This would be my philosophy, and fuck anybody else. They could follow along, if they could keep up.

But it's important to remember that I love my wife. I love this place. Our life here.

He looks into his glass.

"What?" I say.

"Nothing."

"What?"

○

Mostly, I taught them to communicate. To move beyond grunts and text messages. I taught them the mathematics of comma splices and dangling modifiers and inclusive language. I showed them how to parse an argumentative paragraph, how to be assertive, how to slowly, slowly get a reader to think just the way they do. How to control disposition, which is what I did to them.

But mostly, there was no place for cognitive theory, for experimental literature or abstract discourse. The university did Sireen a favor, handing me introduction-to-composition classes after they hired her.

○

"Nothing." He forces a smile. He's got the face here of his entire country. Sometimes, he still has to ask me what certain words mean. He'd never had a funnel cake until Sireen and I bought him one. A corn dog. Cotton candy. I shoved him down the curly slide, at the state fair, and he nearly broke his ankle. He paid for all three of us to go.

"Drink your bourbon," he says.

"Why *are* we drinking it?"

Each glass costs as much as a regular tab.

He sees something in it, staring at it, that I don't. It is possible, like now, to occupy a subject position in discourse and be nothing but an object.

"Never mind. Just drink it."

So I do. And I take another cigarette without asking.

"Chimping looks like good business," I say. Something else to talk about.

"No doubt," he says.

By mentioning it, I give him the opportunity to turn around and have a look at the bar, which is not where chimping technically exists. But it is the last place where it existed for us, which makes it an extension of self. We are more than the meat in our heads. Dimitri and I, right now, are this entire bar.

You see?

The first researchers to work with ontogenetic mapping were psycho-linguists. My dissertation director had been one of them, when he was my age. They studied the intersection of language and cognition. Of language and everything. It became possible to index linguistic tendencies among the neurologically disturbed, which made it possible to begin studying how those tendencies are sourced. Language delineates or creates most "thoughts," and it implies a constructed world.

These are the things I had to learn, to earn my Ph.D. Perception as creation. *Fiat lux.*

What we—they—eventually learned is that you can parse an entire person by indexing his or her probabilistic lingual deep structures. The existential urges, needs, or intentions "beneath" anything he or she says.

Which is the wrong way to think about it, but still.

It became possible to detect early signs, early psycho-linguistic ontogenetic trajectories. Which meant we learned to avoid and appropriately medicate neurological imbalances. It took a while, and we—they—got better at it. Faster.

We'd cured crazy. Or, at least, indexed it. I was ten years old by the time the technology made it into the public schools. Health workers began ontogenetically indexing us with child-sized goggles. We were allowed to watch cartoons while the software marked our dispositions toward neurological imbalance. Anything over five percent sent us into federally mandated therapy at children's psychiatry clinics. The costs were underwritten by the government, and it saved the healthcare giants a fortune.

I never showed any signs, but some of my friends did. They said it was fun, learning to be normal. Playing games with goggles and electroencephalographic hats.

Really, a self is just a matrix of cognitive associations. Learned behaviors, tastes, opinions. Conditioned fears and culturally imparted memories. A person, like Dimitri, is his bread lines and military service and worthless currency.

And with a complete enough series of progressive cognitive indices, with a more-or-less full ontogenetic trajectory, you had a person. Theoretically, if you could activate this data, you could simulate an entire other person, not just the fucked up obsessions and tics we condition away.

Such licensing rights are in the promissory note. Put there to sell what belongs to the moneylenders—to research institutions, originally.

I watch them chimp at the bar. They wiggle and twitch and have a good old time. Those disturbances, free with purchase.

CHAPTER FOUR

"What'd you teach?" Rosie says.

"English," I say.

He has a copy of a local arts circular rolled up in his fist, like a baton. It's called *The Mountainist*. I read it sometimes at the bar, if I'm alone—gardening, music, local politics. I wouldn't have pegged Rosie as a reader.

He tucks it into one of his drawers and hands me a pair of canvas gloves and a litter picker.

"To foreigners?" he says.

"What?"

"Like, illegals?"

My Renewal suit is heavy, and it sticks to my skin. I can already feel the chafing.

"No. English—writing and literature."

He crosses his arms, and his chair pops as he reclines. He has satisfied himself.

"You married?" he says.

"Yes."

"Kids?"

"No."

He points to the window. Outside, there is a white school bus in the lot—an old kind. Diesel engine, security windows. There is a trailer with a portable toilet affixed to the back bumper.

"See you at 3:00," he says.

○

The driver halts the bus ten miles outside of town, along Interstate 26. He is protected from us by security glass and a wire cage.

Our wardens get out of their jump seats. They rode backwards, staring at us. There are twenty workers on this crew, and the wardens gesture us to our feet. The older workers brace themselves on the benches to stand. The young, the belligerent, make a point of rising slowly.

One warden heads out of the bus with his shotgun. The other stands in the aisle.

"You pick one piece of trash at a time," he says. "Paper, plastic. You find metal or glass, you stop and raise your hand. If we see you with it, that's an extra day on your record."

They wanded us, back at the dispatch lot, before we entered the bus. They found a pocket knife on one of the men, and he was ushered at gunpoint into Rosie's office.

"You need to piss, you raise your hand. You get tired, raise your hand. Don't squat or kneel unless you're unconscious. You'll get fresh sun block at lunch."

○

There is an SUV on the shoulder of the highway. Our bus, which catches up to us every fifteen minutes or so, pulls ahead of the vehicle and stops. There are children in the SUV with their hands against the windows. Staring, learning. Their mother holds a tire iron as we approach. One of the back tires is flat.

Our wardens don't acknowledge the woman, but the bus driver gets out and talks to her. He is a large man, and he moves as slowly as we do.

I skip over a scrap of tin foil in the grass in favor of a plastic drinking bottle. The weight of my litter satchel has become organic, like a tumor or a torn ligament. It pulls at my shoulder steadily, building pain. I am not permitted to switch the satchel to the other side until the wardens blow the whistle to do so.

The driver shouts two names into our crew. We all stop to see. They do as they're told, and the rear warden makes them dump their litter gear before they approach the SUV.

The mother is slender, blonde. The two men, from our crew, are black. The only black men on the crew today. They change her tire while the driver fingers his sidearm.

I find spent shotgun shells in a pile. Metal and plastic. I have to raise my hand.

○

There are some things I can't explain. Sireen has her own Ph.D., has written her own papers, is (in many ways) smarter than I am.

Yet, when we go somewhere, I drive. We divide our household duties along mythic lines. Other people, other cultures, once created gods to keep household identity straight. They projected the hearth, the home, and killing other people into the stars. Into the hills. Into anyplace strange enough to be something else.

We still know those ancient rites. I mow the yard. Clean the dishes. Handle things that involve manual tools, like screwdrivers, or bow saws, or kits for fitting gas caps with protective locks. She uses her hands, kneading flat bread or pizza dough. Tucks her fingers between folds of softened fabric. Puts things in old wooden drawers.

When we leave town, like now, we no longer go to spend money. We aren't hunting for antiques, or exploring new restaurants, or drinking familiar beers in strange pubs. Now, when we leave, it's simply to walk someplace new. To hike new trees—any trees at all. It's cheap.

We're driving west, crossing a river into what remains of the Qualla Boundary, the Cherokee land trust, where we will hike upon earth with its own history.

The highway is litter-free.

"Did Dimitri tell you about his article?" Sireen says.

I take the opportunity to glance at her bronzed knee, where it escapes her cargo shorts. She almost looks like one of them, where we're going, those Cherokee. The sun is in her eyes while I watch what the car's wave motions do to her body. We dip and lift differently, sitting a foot apart, and it draws the eye.

"What?"

She looks at me, turning that sun my direction. "At the bar?"

"Which article?"

"He had another one accepted."

"Jesus. That's, what? This year?"

"Three. He said he might buy you a drink, to celebrate."

"Right."

She sees a house alongside a lake as we skirt a roadway levy. These days, we see houses. We construct worlds based on how our distributed neural networks source "need." A house has become primary. Abstractly, it thinks us, and we have become territorial. We protect Sireen's credit rating like our young, for it is the only one we have.

I look across her cheekbones, the gleam of everything on her skin. But I don't see that house. She's smiling. Always. Even when she isn't.

Why are you smiling? I said. I had a hand up over my eyes, just so I could see her doing it against the sun. There were tiny, flesh-toned opals of sweat on her lip. On mine, too, where they didn't feel like opals.

I'm not, she said.

But she was. She always was. Sometimes even when she was sleeping.

You're crazy, I said. It's fucking hot. It was a booster sale, for her graduate student association. Raising money for some new kind of something the university wouldn't pay for. Even back then.

But it's working, she said. The university should have just paid for it, instead of watching me help Sireen sell second-hand books in an overflow parking lot. Her friends stood around other tables, doing their own sweating for the departmental good.

We'd put up flyers. Summer sessions were a tough time to get people's attention on campus.

She kissed me. Connecting sweat and heatflesh. I wiped my lip unconsciously, afterward, and she traced a finger across my cheekbone, like wiping a tear.

I faked a smile, just to keep up.

○

There are signs when you get close to the Boundary that say "Welcome." But that's not what they're trying to say.

Most of the tourist shops along the main avenue have closed. The casino still operates, but we haven't gone. Primarily because you can't drink in there. But plenty of other people go. It still does good business.

We pass young men in parking lots, day laboring in their own city. Standing, smoking. There are more signs, more posters and handbills, printed in the tribe's native language than there used to be. The dances and outdoor productions and traditional games don't attract crowds anymore. The Tribal Council used to organize such things, to correct the discourse regarding tribal identity. While turning a small profit.

The churches still operate. The schools are still open. Smooth-skinned, shirtless boys, white and Indian, play footbag in the yard, basketball on the blacktop. Girls gather in groups, to legislate how things are going. How to present themselves. How to get away with what needs doing. Some smoke in clandestine pockets, but no one cares, least of all the teachers, who are inside, out of the heat, doing anything else.

People wander around the town—the jobless, like a horde. Later, they will cook frozen Renewal Welfare-issued lasagnas, or meals-in-a-box, or local bear meat—still herbed all these traditional years with sumac. They will find things to do, primarily in small groups, the same way we do, back in our town. They will talk about what they haven't found yet—work, hope: a way to share the Depression—which is not what Sireen and I do because it would be a one-sided conversation.

Ours is the only car in the small, graveled lot at the trail head when we get there. You're supposed to put $5 in the padlocked entry-fee box. The money goes toward keeping up the trail, but there's no one here to check.

We hold hands as we walk between basswoods and pitch pines and black walnut trees. We walk among so many nameless things. It's cheap, hiking. And it brings us together. A pursuit we've loved since grad school, when we had even less money than we do now.

"I think I need something," I say.

"Like what?" Sireen says, looking elsewhere. You never look at each other when you're hiking. There's too much to see. Animal awareness. You talk into the distance.

"To do. Other than therapy and Renewal."

"That's a good idea."

I look anyway—I look at her legs, at the camber of her shins and the just-visible veins behind her knees. I can see scars, like granite chips, on the bulbs of her ankles, where, at some point, she has cut herself shaving.

"What would you do?" she says.

"I don't know. Volunteer."

"You should," she says. There is a swing to our arms now. Our handclasp is a fulcrum, dappled by the sunlight through green things. Her ponytail brushes the backs of her shoulders with the same swing, and I wish it could come far enough—just enough—to touch my shoulders, too. A touch she doesn't even control. A natural phenomenon.

"Maybe volunteer teaching. Writing and such," I say.

"Teach who?"

"Whoever. The public."

Her smile becomes difficult. "What will they do with a writing class? They don't have jobs."

She doesn't resist when I lead us off the trail, up a confetti slope, where last fall's dead leaves still pile the earth.

"It's not about them," I say.

She watches the ground now. "I'm sorry. It's a good idea, Ben."

This is it. Light and air and how shoulders look, outside. The flush on her skin is everything. It's important to remember that I love my wife. Our lives here. It's important to remember that we are not in charge.

CHAPTER FIVE

TECHNICALLY, "VISUAL" RHETORIC COUNTED. IT WAS PART of the curriculum—something worth teaching, during introductions to rhetoric and composition because it communicated the principles of presentation and design. There are visual sciences behind this. The eye moves to things in threes. You're not supposed to use positive and negative spaces in halves. You're supposed to carve your space according to the golden mean, a spiral, mapping the image, page, whatever with the interstices of classical aesthetics. Points of maximum visual strike. It's the principle behind constellations.

I didn't teach any of them that this parallels principles of consciousness like motivated perception, revisionist memory, semantic priming. Because they wouldn't get it anyway.

But the artists are wrong. The eye *is* drawn to halves. To symmetry. When we wandered plains and savannahs and scrub-bushed basins, we learned to look first at things that appeared the same on both sides of a vertical axis. Because that's exactly how it looked when something larger, something hungrier was giving you *the* look. An eye per side, a nostril, an ear.

Like I said, everything begins by making the audience pay attention. Giving them attention is giving them awareness. Being. Life itself.

○

Designing an advertisement is a good example.

No one attends concerts advertised only in delicate, serif fonts. Unless the text is blocked and used as an element of design itself. No one attends debates, votes for presidents, or stops motor vehicles.

No one attends free lectures on university-level introduction to rhetoric and composition, in Sentinel Park, Tuesday afternoon— all welcome.

So I used a stencil of a chimpanzee, from an online database, and placed my ad in *The Mountainist*. Small-block Arial in the bottom left third of the page. Something stimulating—popular. Revolutionary.

○

"Everything begins by making your audience pay attention," I say.

There are eleven of them, here in Sentinel Park, listening. During the last few days, while Sireen and I waited for the first day of class, she maintained delicate interest in the idea. She asked questions and offered suggestions. She brought home reams of paper and notepads and red pens from her department's supply closet—none of which, we knew, I would use. We both knew there was no point to this.

Nearby, a solitary Renewal worker sweeps the concrete. I don't see his warden anywhere.

"Communication is not a social endeavor," I say. "When you speak—or write—to an audience, you project yourself. You become both subject and object because you must *extend* yourself into a position of understanding what you are saying."

They are not understanding what I am saying. They are squinting into the overcast glow, leaning forward or backward on their cement slabs. Trying to be comfortable.

"Think of it like this," I say: "each of us understands *understanding*. We know what it is to read or listen or watch and *get* the message, but we don't know—can't know—how this experience goes for others. It's phenomenology."

No response. Like reptiles, out for the light and the heat. Only accidentally in class. They find themselves here—in any classroom—because it just happened. Not for a good reason.

"So, when you speak or write or perform," I say, "you construct your message for *yourself*."

One of them is not leaning. She sits upright, in that way, that posture that somehow girls learn. Sireen sits the same way. I barely notice the others around this girl—fallen pillars on their amphitheater slabs. She raises a caryatid arm, dreadlocks like fingers of blonde stone across her shoulders. It is sculptural hair, a doll's hair—the best stone carvers can do.

"Yes?" I say.

"But others respond to what we say," she says. "What is the difference between actually communicating with someone and only imagining yourself doing it?"

"What is your name?"

"Zoe."

Zoe is in her early twenties. She wears oversized sunglasses, distressed leggings, and expensive shoes. Likely, she's a trustafarian, living in one of these condos downtown. Pretending in that way that goes well beyond simply simulating poverty. Because for whatever fucking reason, destitution is fashionable.

"Look, Zoe: you create your message to make sense for the audience—really, the message creates itself, and 'you' have nothing to do with it, but never mind."

She blinks her sculptural eyelids. Slowly, like erosion.

"The audience that you imagine, the audience's *understanding* that you imagine, is based on your own. It's based on your previous experiences. You can never experience your audience's minds, so you're always communicating with yourself."

"So there is no difference?"

"Not really."

"You said we have to make the audience pay attention," she says.

"Everything begins that way."

"Well." She crosses her arms. Her bra is darker than her shirt, which is not something I should notice. "How does imagining ourselves make others pay attention?"

"Are you paying attention?" I say.

○

I watch Zoe file out with the others, back up the steps, into the real world. She has moved beyond view when I hear a motorcycle engine start.

One of the other students approaches me, at the bottom.

"Dr. Cade?" he says.

"Yes?"

"Could you spare a dollar?"

○

Cynthia is behind me. I am in her office, reclining on her therapeutic sofa, which doubles as a medical device. I lie here, field dressed by the sofa's built-in diagnostic wires. It listens to my heartbeat. It measures my respiration. It touches my brow delicately with sanitary adhesion-pad fingertips. It gives me what I need through a polyvinyl umbilicus inserted into my wrist. I see what I'm supposed to—which seems to be this room, unaffected— through the sofa's elastic goggles.

Change blindness. She will make sure I don't see what I'm not supposed to see.

Cynthia is nothing but a warm voice in the darkness. The sedative she has given me through the sofa creates sensations of wave motion. I am tidal, and only later will I experience the motion sickness that repossession therapy causes.

"Do you want me to think?" I say. "Should I try to . . . summon ideas?"

"No, Ben."

I can hear the smile in her voice. The patience. She's a psychiatrist—I wonder how much student debt she carries. How much she's paid for this.

"Why don't you tell me a story," she says. "About graduate school. Something you enjoyed."

"If I tell you this story, will I lose it?"

"Parts of it. It might feel like someone else's story. As if you can't remember if you experienced it or heard about it."

I don't believe her. Memory is not an act of recall, it is an act of creation. We create ourselves, every moment, in our own image.

But it doesn't matter.

"All right," I say. "The most difficult course I took, during my doctoral program, was simply called 'Syntax.' It was taught by the director of my program. He was a theoretical syntactician, a psycholinguist. One of those who developed the ideas behind the indexing technology."

"He sounds brilliant," Cynthia says.

"Syntax was exactly what it sounds like—a survey of models for explaining how language can mean anything, how its mathematics transcend vocal and aural abstraction and *move*, within the very materials of our brains.

"But you must understand," I say, "my director is a very gregarious person. He's a great fan of poetry, of people, of anything that means anything to anyone. He's funny."

I can hear Cynthia smile across the wine-dark sea. The sofa cushions deflate ever so slightly beneath me.

I am sinking.

"I was near the top of my class—there had been nothing he had introduced that I didn't, after some effort, finally understand.

"But eventually, there was. One of my classmates asked my director to explain the concepts behind his formative theory of syntax. So, he did. He taught it slowly—he wrote everything on the chalkboard."

"A chalkboard?"

"He preferred them."

"Go on."

"With each new piece of his masterwork, he would turn, he would watch. He checked to make sure that we were following along. One by one, fewer and fewer of us were able to follow him. Fewer of us were able to associate ideas the way he did. And as he went further, as he tried to reveal the deep structures of this theory, this theory that explains our most basic, our most primary of abstractions—language itself—he spoke less to us and more to himself. He stopped checking to see if we were following along. I remember looking around at my classmates and watching them, like divers too long under the water. I could see when they could no longer see.

"My director filled the chalkboard with linguistic equations. He was sweating as he worked, and there were only two or three of us who were still following. Who still deserved to be his students."

"Go on."

"He had nearly filled the chalkboard, but he wasn't finished, so he picked up another piece of chalk and began finishing his equation by writing on the brick wall beside the board, clutching the chalk like a charred stick, like he was cave painting. He wrote with both hands at the same time. It was beautiful."

"Go on."

"Then I felt pressure on my eyelids, like staring at a strobe light. I looked at his mosaic, at everything he'd written. I looked at my notes. They were nonsense. I had no idea how he'd gotten from the beginning to the end. I was lost, and so were the other two students—the last two. I knew, then, for the first time, that I simply wasn't smart enough. I felt calm. For the first time all semester.

"It felt much the way I feel now."

"Why do you think that is?"

I think about the truth.

"I don't fucking know."

○

"Do you feel different?" Sireen says.

"I feel hung over."

"What happened?"

"I don't really remember."

I finished vomiting hours ago. We are lying in bed, beneath only a sheet. Because it's hot. Sireen has it pulled down to her hips, and I watch how the moon's blue light makes her skin seem violet, her breasts wine-dark.

We are nothing but our entire lives here. I still feel calm—an aftereffect of the chemicals and sedatives Cynthia administered earlier. I think of Sireen's skin in the sunlight, in the woods, and I wish we could build our house there. Around a tree, like Odysseus.

She touches my neck, and I concentrate. This is how I contribute now. How I build a better life, family, place to be. Trading myself for our good.

It's important to remember that I love her.

I'd made a friend.

Ben, he said, finally. The bar was crowded when I arrived. There were pictures on the walls of the campus architecture. Which was looming just outside.

He was another taciturn alcoholic. From my program, studying poetry. He knew Sireen, which darkened him. He had written poetry about how she didn't love him and why this was the same thing as something more meaningful, like science.

Meet Sireen, he said.

She rolls over beside me. Brings those breasts against my ribcage. Divots her chin into my shoulder.

"I read the doctor's literature," she says. Quiet. Straight into my skin. "About collateral memory damage."

We met when she was drunk and beautiful. Arms and legs in unsteady arcs.

"To anything that pertains," I say.

Ben, Sireen said, extending a hand languidly from her seat. Sit down. She still had an accent then.

My friend put Sireen's hand in mine, to shake, because she was too drunk to coordinate it herself. He said, She's another one from the math group—

Non-positively curved geometry, Sireen said.

One of Sireen's neighbors, a woman, leaned into her. You look positively curved to me, darling! They laughed.

Can I buy you a drink? I said.

You know, Sireen said, I can predict your future with statistical theory. Her eyes widened, as if she'd impressed herself.

My friend brought us drinks. Ben, I found out about the   , he said.   '   -

"I pertain," Sireen says. We slip where she's pressed against me, sweating like condensation. "Grad school was us. Beginning."

One semester, Sireen's program got to her. It was too much, and she exhausted herself. We had to put her in the hospital, and she took incompletes for all of her classes. I took care of her, afterward, in her tiny apartment. I gave her everything she needed, and she fell in love for good.

> She laid on the sheets. The summer's blue night louvered through uneven blinds. Naked against the heat. The sheets were topographic around us. Too soon. She wasn't better yet. Wasn't finished becoming worse. I was still worried about never-ending theories.

She lips a whisper against my skin. "What will you forget?"
"It's all I can do, Sireen."
"I know," she says.

> I'm sorry, she said.

"I'm sorry."

CHAPTER SIX

I HAVE TO WAIT A LONG TIME BEFORE ROSIE TURNS ON THE light and summons me inside. Ten minutes. I don't have anything to do, anything to read, standing there, so I listen to other workers converse quietly. We're getting used to each other.

When the light comes on, two young men, the ones who changed the white woman's tire along the highway, emerge at once. I have never seen Rosie admit more than one worker at a time. They give me a good look, and I give it back, as if, eventually, we will learn to read each other's minds. We might as well practice now.

Rosie closes the windowless door behind his desk when I walk in. He moves piles of newspapers and circulars from his desk to the floor.

"You saw the rockslide on the news?" Rosie says.

West of town, in the mountains. It crippled the entire highway, and the expected repair costs are beyond both the state and the federal budgets. The newscasters reported talks with foreign investors to finance the work. Renewal from three states will absorb fifty percent of the workload.

"Yes," I say.

Rosie grins. "You get to break rocks," he says. "Just like old times."

He enters some information into his computer, points at the thumbprint scanner. I put my thumb in place, checking in. There are six other workers waiting in line outside.

"But it isn't all bad," he says. "Two of your hours are just sitting in the bus. There and back."

"Yes, sir," I say.

"That big Methodist church downtown donated protein bars. Charity. You'll get one at lunch." He pulls one out of a drawer and unwraps it.

"Yes, sir." I look at the floor as I turn around. We're having herbed rice and beans for dinner tonight. Sireen promised.

"Cade," Rosie says.

I stand in front of the door and stare at my co-workers outside through the window. They watch, in line.

"You know, I never went to college," he says.

He puts down the protein bar when I turn around. I can only see his eyes above the rim of his monitor.

"You know," I say, "I'm teaching a free course downtown. Writing, communication—that sort of thing."

"Is that what you're doing."

It isn't a question.

○

There is a mansion in town. You can see it from the highway on your way into the mountains, where it seems small. Before, you could pay $40 to tour the inside. Learn the domestic secrets of the magnate who built it during the Gilded Age. When Civil War Reconstruction made white men rich. When they hired the men we'd freed.

For $20 less, you could drive your car around the grounds, but you couldn't get out. There used to be hundreds of acres of vineyards. There used to be guest houses and small hotels, done in the same style. You could visit during Christmas as a special event.

Now, it is a club. People play golf upon the old vine beds. They swim and get massages and wave at the armed security guards on their ways in and out.

The bus driver takes us off the highway, along the exit where the state's brown road signs used to identify the mansion as a cultural destination. The rockslide is still fifty miles west, along the highway.

We look at each other, at our wardens. No one says anything as the mansion's security guards wave us through the front gate. We park behind a service building, where there is also a catering truck.

You don't get the same wardens every time. Like the crews, they rotate, along with the driver.

The wardens stand. I can see our driver out of my window when he exits the cab. A man in a suit greets him—hands him an envelope—and the driver pulls money out of it. He starts counting.

"Anyone here want to file a complaint?" one of the wardens says.

We look away, hoping like students that they won't call on us.

"The alternative is to break rocks in the hills," the other warden says.

"You'll be given rubber shoes to wear in the kitchen. Don't touch them without permission. We see you bend over, that's another day on your record."

The driver is satisfied. He signals the wardens.

"Now, when we call your name, say 'here.'" He pulls a small notepad out of his pocket. The other one is holding the worker manifest that Rosie brought him before we left.

"Cade?"

"Here."

Now they know. Whom to go after, if this gets out.

I wait while they take attendance.

○

Because I am the only one in the bar, because it is 12:15 in the afternoon—because I ordered hard liquor, the bartender is letting me chimp for free. Again. She's good. A professional. Asks no questions. Which is why I had to ask her myself, for the goggles. I only have so much money for the afternoon, and drinks are important. Dimitri and Sireen are both at work. It's Thursday, after all. She won't be home until after dinner, which is to say, after our usual dinnertime, because she has a department meeting. Dinner is now whenever she gets home, not when we get hungry. Spaghetti tonight, which I'm good at.

This is important. The meeting is important. Her department has to figure out what to do with its vacant position.

I'm not taking any chances this time. I'm already in the booth—I will not look at that carpet again while wearing these goggles. Apparently, sims have settings. Difficulty levels, which Dimitri didn't tell me about. It also has networking capability. This bar offers access for free.

I'm curious. I enable the network and set the difficulty level to its lowest. There is a tiny adjustment wheel on one of the earpieces. I need to see compulsion again. Obsession. I'm not interested in hallucinations or perversion. The menu offers thousands of available simulations.

I sit still, quietly disturbed, and drink.

○

What I'm seeing are feet. That is to say, the images appearing in my mind's eye are feet. Mental seeing and vision are not connected, and there is no such thing as the mind's eye.

But whatever.

The sim keeps stimulating disconnected images, none of which I care to see. Particularly annoying are the feet, which is why I think I keep seeing them. I'm looking down at them, as if they are my own—at the flip-flops they're wearing.

A network-connection request appears in my field of vision. I approve it.

These flip-flops piss me off. They spin like synchronized propellers—their axes are the flip-flop support straps, which divide the large toe and the one beside it. I can't control the image. I can't make them stop. It is ridiculous, but watching, but counting. It doesn't make me feel good. It keeps me from feeling bad.

I hear a woman's voice through the goggles' earphones. When I glance at the TV behind the bar, I get a reprieve from the flip-flops. The TV is muted.

"Authorities from the Center for Civic Renewal and the Downtown Chamber of Commerce believe the movement is tied to recent trends in social experimentation," she says. Her voice sounds digitized.

The bartender is in the back. I am alone.

"Leah Johnson, a senior poverty studies major at Central, leads a field team surveying grassroots governance—"

"Hello?" I say. Out loud.

I decide to ignore the flip-flops, which creates a sensation of nausea.

"—the unemployed or underemployed under 30."

"Hey," I say.

"Yes?" she says.

"What are you doing?"

"What do you want?"

"Who are you?" I say.

"Who are *you*?"

"Ben."

The bartender is back. She ignores me. Ignoring the flip-flops isn't working. I wonder whose feet these were. Whose life of hell. It is an asinine simulation, an introduction, the result of setting the difficulty to minimal.

"Really?" she says.

"Yes, really."

"You shouldn't give out your real name."

"Oh."

"Hold on," she says. "Thirty percent chance of rain. For this time of year, we are at positive two inches. Northern Georgia and the Piedmont, meanwhile, are still struggling with a now ninety-day drought.

"That's better," she says.

"What are you chimping?" I say. "Why are you telling me the news?"

"I'm not telling *you* anything, and it's none of your business."

"Right." I need another drink anyway, and my head is starting to hurt. I've had enough.

"What are *you* chimping?" she says.

"Fuck you."

〇

Attendance has grown. They sit clustered, in a stadium rectangle—up the rows, into the air. They have grouped themselves against the others in Sentinel Park. Like a class. Those from the first day are sitting in roughly the same places, as if identified there.

Just like real students.

I can tell they are in the same places because Zoe is in the same place. She is wearing a sundress today, a blue one, and her dreads are bound against the top of her head.

They—someone—brought me something to write on. There at the bottom of the amphitheater, where the answers lie, where we always speak the truth from below, is an easel. It is duct-taped in places, but there is a large pad of bound newsprint upon it.

There are at least twenty of them now.

Up here, on the sidewalk. People stare.

○

"So, why do I say that ethos is the most important?" I say.

Some of them are taking notes. A few smoke cigarettes. Most just stare, underwhelmed. I am the weakest of this afternoon's street performers.

"Because," one of them says, "we have to believe what you're saying?"

"I can make you believe using logical data," I say, "or I can manipulate you into doing so with pathos."

"I don't know then."

"I said everything begins by making the audience pay attention."

The policeman, up on the street level, where the sidewalk chessboards and hotdog vendors are, is paying attention. He watches us without moving.

"Will logic make you pay attention?" I say.

No.

"Will pathos?"

No. They think they know how to play the academically loaded question game.

"Of course it will," I say. "I can certainly make you pay attention if I can manipulate your emotions. Who earns more handouts? An able-bodied transient, or one without legs, injured in the war?"

"Then what?" Zoe says.

"It's because," I say, "ethos is the only one of the three that belongs to *you*. Pathos and logos reside with the speaker. Ethos is your idea of why, how, or to what extent I should be believed."

One of them turns around and looks at the cop. Intuitive. I've seen him with Zoe, before and after class. David? Something.

"What did I say, before, about speaking?" I say.

"We're only ever talking to ourselves," David says, returning his attention to the class. The cop has wandered off.

"So if ethos belongs to you," I say, "how do I manipulate it?"

I motion for a cigarette from one on the first row. He gives it hurriedly.

They are quiet. Cars move, people chat on the sidewalks above, or in the empty space around our classroom.

Finally: "You don't?" Zoe says.

"Which is why it's the most important—the most dangerous. I want what's yours, but you cannot give it to me, so I will do everything I can to make it an advantage, not a weakness."

"Including deception?"

"Of course. Now, hand in your introductory essays."

○

"You didn't bring your essay?"

"I did it," Zoe says. "It's just not here."

Of course. *Can I run back to my dorm room? My computer froze. No, I don't have a copy.*

"Come see," she says.

○

Recruitment is a discipline unto itself. Governments, revolutions, and religions know this. It is an application of rhetoric—how to align someone's disposition with an ideal, an action, which is usually anathema to personal fulfillment. How do you convince a suicide bomber? How do you sell laundry detergent? How do you sell university enrollment?

You don't. Nothing can be described, nothing portrayed or sold, in any fashion that induces action. You sell, instead, a world without your product. You sell longing and regret, which are cheap. You sell hindsight, insurance—which is nothing but a life without.

Which is why, then—when they made us recruiters, when they forced faculty to turn away from their articles, and conferences, and evening dinners—it didn't work. Enrollment is everything. The university needed more money. More students. More promises. And what is life without education? Never mind repossession, loss of self, being less than all you can be, writ large and terrifying. Universities employ salespeople whose job it is to sell un-education, to recruit. But they could only do so much. So the administration made us do it, too. Applied rhetoric. Education in action. Correcting perception.

The first of many small losses of self.

But the initiative came late in the term—handed down in departmental meetings I didn't attend. Because I already knew. I was already giving out "A"s because why the hell not? The sciences were exempt—they were forced to secure more grants. To fund a better fertilizer, a new math, or cheaper bombs.

I dialed the phone number printed on my register. Someone, somewhere. Adjusted my earpiece.

"May I speak to [name]?" I said.

"It's pronounced [name]."

"My apologies. I've argued for IPA transcriptions."

"What?"

"May I speak to [name]? This is Dr. Cade from Central University."

"Oh! Yes. Hold on."

Muted scrambling. The university. Yes, to you!

"Hello."

"Hello, [name]. This is Dr. Cade from Central University. I'd like to talk to you about our languages and cultural studies program."

"Okay."

"This conversation may be recorded for training purposes. Is that all right, [name]?"

"Sure."

"Have you chosen a university yet?"

"No."

"Don't."

"What?"

"Don't. Particularly not this one."

"What?"

"Do you know anything about HVAC repair or installation?"

"What is that?"

"What about locksmithing?"

"Like, picking locks?"

"Both of these professions earn more money than I do. Enjoy greater job security. Do you have a new car, [name]?"

"No."

"Do you want one? Nice clothes? An apartment with granite counter-tops?"

"Sure, I guess."

"Do you know what an aircraft marshaller is, [name]? It's the person who use neon wands to wave planes in and out of terminal gates."

"Ok."

"They're very important, [name]. An essential service, like plumbing. It's a good trade, but I can teach you the secrets of consciousness, being, and the existential nature of language, here at Central University. Would you like me to teach you these things, [name]?"

"I guess so."

"Fuck you, [name]. Have a nice day."

◌

I follow Zoe out of the park. A few students stop me, here and there, on the stairs. Shaking hands, saying thanks. *Can I make up the first assignment?*

Up top, at street-level, I follow Zoe. It's awkward: my artificial student-essays and notes clutched against my chest, walking single-file—at least David took the newsprint and promised to bring it back, so I wouldn't have to carry it out of the park. There isn't enough room on the sidewalk to walk abreast. Transients and children and people in distribution lines take up most of the pavement. Zoe seems to know every tenth person.

Sireen sends me a text message. **Finished? How'd it go?**

"Still back there?" Zoe says.

Someone must have handed Zoe a cup of coffee. A cup of something. She holds it at a right angle to her chest, looking at her shoulder, which, in this context, stands in for me. Turning to look at me fully would mean colliding with something in front of her. This is how we source gaze. Only, she owns hers. Young, female, liberated. I am male, and I know enough gender theory that I have been trained to be ashamed of mine.

In this instance, she is substituting me for the tiny hairs—soft blonde—standing on her polished scapula. Bright white in the sun. Easier and safer to see than me.

"Yes. Still here."

Coming home? Sireen texts.

"Good," Zoe says. "It's not far."

Soon, I text. **Chatting with some of the students.**

"Good," I say.

Love you.

Zoe walks us across the street, between pedi-cabs and smart cars. The architecture casts parallelograms, trapezoid shadows—its faces and finials and loft-apartments. We watch police on foot patrol. There is screaming somewhere in the arts district.

"So how did you come up with this idea?" Zoe says.

We walk abreast now.

"The assignment?"

"The class."

"I didn't invent class, Zoe."

She adjusts a free-hanging dread as we make a turn. We're off-street now, between and behind buildings. Fire escapes throw new shadows.

"People are talking about you," she says.

"What do they say?"

"The new Socrates. A teacher for the people."

She laughs.

Finally.

"Here it is," Zoe says.

"*This* is your essay?"

"Among other things."

I think about bedroom silence. About the house Sireen and I will buy. How I will spend my evenings quietly, un-educated. A full suppression of identity. By that time, I will have reduced myself to zero, and I won't need beer, or sex, or drugs to do it.

Homeownership. Peace. The fulfillment of all things, our parents tell us. Our government tells us. I think about standing with a student—a woman half my size in a sundress and sandals, five blocks deep into a half-abandoned commercial borough. I think about why people don't turn their essays in on time.

Her essay lies on the concrete. She has written it upon the skin of a young man her age with a black marker. He lies limp against an un-refurbished Art Deco brick foundation. He wears only a pair of black shorts like a dark flag against his pale, hairless skin.

He doesn't move. There is a wheatpaste poster of a chimpanzee slathered onto the bricks above him.

"Among other things?" I say.

"I also needed to create a proposal," Zoe says. "The introductory essay was perfect."

His forehead reads 'Everything begins by making your audience pay attention.'

"What is this proposing?" I say.

She shrugs and lights a cigarette. I motion for one, and she hands it over. I look both ways down the alley.

"Are you going to read it?"

I am her teacher.

"Of course I am," I say. He doesn't look like he's breathing.

I ignore my phone when it vibrates in my pocket.

"Did I get your attention, Dr. Cade?"

"Yes."

"So I'm doing well?"

"Do you think I'm creating the meaning you intended?" I say.

She looks at him. "I don't know."

"Do you think I'm stacking images and unpacking ideas just the way you did, communicating this to yourself?"

"Are you?"

"Probably not."

"I see."

"But Zoe." I touch her shoulder, and she plants her student's gaze back on me. It's different. "I'm paying attention."

CHAPTER SEVEN

Sireen and I go on a home pre-possession tour. It's sponsored by the realtor's office, downtown, with which we have decided to do business. The tour is free, and it includes coffee, croissants, and informative guidebooks with glossy printed photo sheets and professional copy, perfect bound.

At 7:30 AM, we file into a chartered tour bus. Air-conditioned, pneumatic brakes. It rides like a Cadillac. I let Sireen have the window seat. I prefer the aisle, where I can see a hand-made chimpanzee decal stuck to the footboard. The board's rubber ridges have worn free of the sticker—it only exists in the troughs between. A poor-resolution printout from some nature magazine.

Because the tour is full, the bus drives through downtown. The guide describes prominent buildings, explains the architecture. Our town was spared Civil War damage because it is tucked away in the tail-end of the Appalachians. The town went bankrupt later, Art Deco poor, and spent eighty years paying its debts rather than filing for relief. The town lacked money for too long to build anything newer—now, the architecture is culture. Identity. The last seven sitting presidents have all vacationed in its most historic hotel. Enjoyed its hillside golf. Its distant Smoky Mountains.

We skip dangerous parts of town, maneuvering through boroughs. Our first stop is a recently renovated '20s-era bungalow. Its owners defaulted on their home improvement loan, so it is now in short sale. They are fourth-generation owners.

"Are you excited?" Sireen says. She is wearing a sundress today—a rarity. Her position as a professor is better suited to pants. She smiles. The hair on the right side of her forehead moves in the shaft of tubed air blowing from the conical twist-vent overhead. Her hair is down today.

I smile back. The fabric of her dress is thin between my palm and her thigh. It is pale against her skin. The next few days on her ovulation calendar are important. She told me before we left. It thrums her, every time, even if it hasn't worked yet, and I can see it in everything she does. The statistics and calculation of it.

"Yes."

I am.

Every home on this tour is either in short sale or has been foreclosed upon. Our realtor is only one branch of a national franchise. It offers signed affidavits from every bank that owns a property on this tour. Short sale offers are guaranteed a response within fourteen days, and the banks are prepared to accept up to 40% losses, should appraisal values not match asking price. Several inspection firms are also partnered in this pyramid. Ready to go.

The bungalow sits at the top of a hill in a mixed neighborhood. There are tenement apartments and rent-controlled houses about a mile away. But that no longer means what it used to mean.

It is a red brick house with white trim. It boasts a study with original windows and molding. Bookshelves.

Sireen looks forward. She is five houses ahead, in the guidebook.

○

We tour our lives together in these houses. It is a fast and easy way to spend the early part of the day. Living ahead of oneself in a place one doesn't—could—own. The selling points of our futures together, in these places, appear in clean, bold font in our guide. WINTER VIEWS OF THE MOUNTAINS. Sireen in her bare feet—pads of feminine skin against the STAINED CONCRETE. She wears one of my shirts, taking a break for a glass of water from the CUSTOM FILTRATION SYSTEM. She brines Thanksgiving turkeys overnight in a five-gallon bucket that we keep in the MUDROOM, OR SOLARIUM. Will keep. She grades papers in her study, wearing sweat pants and faded alma mater T-shirts. She complains about her committee, a fully fluted glass of pinot in one hand, her anger in the other.

She spins past the ORIGINAL WAINSCOTING in this one, past the CONDITIONED PLASTER in that, her face alight with tenure. Publication. A new course approval. Travel funds.

I see her dirty fingers in these HANGING FLOWERBEDS—her domestic anger between the REFURBISHED BALUSTERS, upstairs. I am on my knees in this half-bath, sick from too much eggnog. It speckles my dark turtleneck. Winks in the lights of our Christmas tree.

A baby cries somewhere.

○

There are two houses left on the tour, but this one is only three blocks from where we live, so we're done. We've seen enough. We hide in a pass-through closet while everyone else vacates the premises. We are having a good time, skipping out. In grad school, after we'd started dating, we would cut classes to meet for shots of house whiskey at the campus bar. We would kiss it from each other's lips, like drinking bitters to remedy some discomfort caused, really, by drinking too much. When I could, I would press the bulb of my upper lip against her teeth, when that smile climbed. Because I could. We would spend our student loan disbursements on cigarettes and small gifts. She likes chocolate.

> I liked how it made her bounce around the room, when she'd had some. I gave her a box, and we each ate one before taking our shots.
>
> Oh, Ben, she said. It's disgusting.
>
> I chased her around the billiards table, just to be obnoxious, and she could barely speak for all the breathing and grinning.
>
> You ruined chocolate, she said.
>
> And whiskey, I said.

CHIMPANZEE

We hold hands down this hallway—a ranch-style. Long and bricked and endless. Quiet walls. The master bedroom is carpeted.

"What do you think?" she says.

"I love you."

"About the house, ass." She slaps. She laughs through white teeth.

"It's fine."

In the bedroom, the light is pale dark.

"I like it."

I can see black walnut leaves through the blinds. Someone else's household dust is still upon the sill. Sireen's hips are strong against mine. The gears and schedules of her flesh. Conception thinks her. Even—especially—here.

"I like all of them," she says.

This is not my home—not our bedroom, with its histories and identities and roles. Its failing duties. *This* house is what I am giving. What I can get. The duty of the contemporary male, who really shouldn't want to provide. It's antiquated. So he gives himself away instead, securing futures. When my father was my age, he spent afternoons in the garage, routing trim or leveling bookshelves. He cut pipe for leaky faucets and showed me how to hold knives. He would do these things on weekends, or after work, when pocketed time made simple crafts meaningful.

I do not own power tools.

I pull Sireen's dress up over her hips. They are alluvial—polished stone in the room-light, dressed with cotton and lace. The shelves of her ribcage open like vents when she lifts her arms.

"I like anything you want," I say.

I mean it.

○

There is empty money in this place—the utilities still function because it must appeal to people like us, even empty, if it is to sell. No one buys a hot house, a stale fridge—a dry toilet. We leave the lights off so no one knows we're here.

The water is hot, thanks to the active gas line and the tankless water heater, which saves the average homeowner a great deal of money, given a long enough timeline. I learned this from our guide book. This shower is lined with Travertine tile, and it is not enclosed. One wall remains open because the rain-flow showerhead, with digital temperature control, does not spray in a wide enough cone to dampen the floor. The shower is large enough that condensation doesn't gather on the telescopic shaving mirror.

Beneath that water, that heat. I am. Some Tibetan meditation on some alpine bluff. A waterfall as God—enlightenment is the pressure of falling things—water, peace, gravity. You try to think of nothing, be nothing, reduce the complications of yourself to something primal. Something that sleeps and fucks, looks askance at natural threats without worrying. No one has a Ph.D. in the shower. No one has sex like a genius.

No one lives in this house.

○

"Are we doing the right thing?" Sireen says.

"Yes," I say. "All we can do is stay smart. Be smarter than the situation."

"It wasn't supposed to go like this," she says.

"What?"

"Like this."

That makes me smile. An old smile. One that belonged to a graduate student in a bar. Angry and loud—opinions about all things. About theory, my director, women. I am the collected lineage of my fathers—the bloodline. The brightest star. My grandfather was a plumber. One of them. The other sold mattresses and grew tomatoes. One of our ancestors fought in the Revolutionary War. I am the brilliant fluid in my mother's belly—the stars and sine waves of her ambitions, first dates, girlhood dolls. What she expected of a son like me.

I am Sireen's childhood dream—the husband she awaited.

"We don't have to do this," she says.

I shouldn't have left her alone in this room, where I couldn't be touched. Laughed with among friends around cheap drinks, sharing ignorance, even that first night in her apartment.

I percuss a finger along the knobs of her spine. Which is absurd. No one *owns* a spine. An elbow. Feelings. There is no *owner* in the mind—no extra-planar ghost steering identity from a magic realm.

Sireen *is* her spine. I am my drumming finger. Selfhood is just the brain behaving, like running is just legs moving.

But she is *my* wife. I feel it, from forehead to groin. It's important to remember that I love her. I have to. There is so much to lose to Cynthia's machines. So much of me tied up in how I became so, with Sireen, studying. The collateral damage is our history—why, for example, I love her at all.

"Yes," I say, "we should do this. It'll be okay."

○

In our own house, in our bed, we don't touch. We source romance with boundaries. A bed is two halves, which are sometimes impenetrable. Space and breathing and unconsciousness of one's own. We must drool and snore and stink on our own halves. We must dampen sheets with natural body oils, at different rates, between linen-washings.

Or else, what is marriage?

A married house is a system of designated spaces, regularly used. Which is how selfhood works. I have to remember. Designated practices, routine patterns. Our homes are what we learned from our parents. Our first house is every house afterward—we measure them all this way. Religious faith is family lineage, not belief. Political party loyalty is the preservation of grandma's Saturday pancakes, uncle's birdhouse collection, father's cancer.

This is what it means to me, buying a house.

You don't sell houses or rhetorical disposition. You sell their lack.

I'm not supposed to write any of this down. During repossession. It's a violation of the agreement. But no one will know. Eventually, not even me.

○

Sometimes, Sireen joins me and Dimitri at the bar. We can buy cigarettes on these occasions because she feels more guilty than I do about taking them from him. About both of us taking them. He gives them to her sometimes on their way to work.

"It's gorgeous," she says, leaning in to me.

Dimitri is a bachelor. He appreciates fine things, like designer aftershave, tailored suits, or original kitchen hardware. He is good at appreciating all things over the rim of his tumbler.

"We're thinking of putting an offer in," she says.

"That's great," he says. Orders a round of the good bourbon. Another celebration.

"It's only a twenty-minute walk from your place," she says. A little drunk.

"Which one?"

"The red-brick bungalow," I say.

"That's fucking fantastic," he says. "You kids."

I drink my bourbon quickly when it comes. Sireen holds my hand under the table.

"It's going to be great," I say.

"Yeah."

"Sounds like."

"Hey," he says, "how's class?"

They both look at me.

"Good, you know. The students listen."

"Seriously?" he says. "I can't get mine to stay awake."

Sireen laughs. Deep, sensual. The female drinking laugh. "Mine are fucking zombies," she says.

"Some of them have given me a nickname," I say.

"Yeah?"

"Socrates. 'An educator for the people.'"

They laugh with me, then we fall silent, watching the waitress negotiate the bar, the crowd. The drinks.

"Hey," he says, "you guys want to chimp?"

Sireen looks at him over her drink. "I don't know," she says.

"It's nothing," Dimitri says.

"I don't know," I say.

He offered us tickets to a forthcoming show, downtown, when we got here. No one we've heard of, but a band he likes.

We told him no.

"Which sim do you have in mind?" Sireen says.

"A new one," he says. "Called 'Jim and Carol.'"

"The fuck?" I say.

"They've more or less perfected it. Entire identities—this couple is codified and indexed and bat-shit crazy in love."

Here we go.

"It's supposed to be intense—in a good way. Like taking X."

"Who will you be?" Sireen says.

"The friend," he says, "over for a visit."

"Okay."

"Okay. Let's do it."

Dimitri orders the goggles. A martini.

○

"I don't want to talk about it."

"That's okay," Cynthia says. She smiles. It's supposed to be for me, but she looks too quickly down into her notes. Smiles at them instead. "We can talk about something else."

○

Rosie orders me onto a stool near the Renewal suits while he checks the others in. He is sending them into the mountains again. I am not going.

The bus leaves. Plainclothes monitors disappear in different directions down the sidewalks, beyond the chain link and razor wire that lines the edge of this lot. One warden remains, and he secures the gates with a padlock.

Rosie is checking his worker manifests against the display on his monitor. From here, I can't see what he sees.

"You're working on the lot today," he says.

"Yes, sir."

He looks up and squints at me, like a stranger in the corner. It takes him a minute to figure things out.

"That means trimming the weeds, hosing off the trailer, etc., etc. There's a list."

"Like chores," I say.

"You think that's funny?"

63

"No, sir."

"I give my son lists of chores," he says. "It's important."

"Yes, sir."

That stops him. He puts his manifest down and swivels his chair. He's got a look in his eyes. A face that sweats in this tepid trailer. He's got a blue denim jacket on the back of his chair. He wears a short-sleeved button-down that exposes a surgical scar along one arm.

I understand. I'm sweating in here, too. This suit.

"Why do you do that?" he says.

"What?"

"'Sir.' All the time 'sir.'"

"I don't know," I say. "You're in charge."

"Did your students call you 'sir?'"

"Some of them."

He stands up and unlocks the door behind his desk. "Come over here," he says. There is no chair beside his desk, so I carry the stool with me across the trailer. There is no light in the room behind the door—I can only see what is incidentally lit by the windows out here. Half of a portable cot, a pile of laundry, rumpled bedding. He steps out of the room with a mason jar and sets two shot glasses on his desk. He is careful how he moves the photo of his kids to make room. I don't see any photos of their mother.

When he goes back to the dark room, he kicks the cot further into the darkness before closing the door and returning to his desk.

Up here, on this stool, I can see when he smiles—I can see the bridgework among his teeth. The false teeth are too bright. Their artificially jaundiced finishes haven't kept up with the natural patina of the real ones.

"You drink?" he says.

"Yes."

He concentrates on removing the lid from the jar. "No 'sir' this time?"

"Well, now we're drinking."

He pours two drinks, and we hold the glasses to our lips, inhaling, like two men sniffing for poison. We are at an impasse until Rosie swallows his.

"That's from the hills," he says.

It's unpleasant.

"One of my monitors found the still," he says.

"Fringe benefits," I say.

"They shot him, right after he got his observation off. Text message."

"Jesus," I say.

"Sweet Jesus," he says.

"How'd you get the jar?"

He pours me another. "We look after our own."

The phone rings on his desk. He ignores it.

"Why'd you pick me for this?" I say.

"You got lots of friends?" he says.

"No."

"Then don't ask stupid questions. A man does what he does."

○

We drink three more shots each. I feel like a bird. Something domestic, perched on this stool over Rosie's desk.

"I been where you are, you know," he says.

"A worker?"

"Yeah."

He has another drink, but he doesn't pour one for me this time.

"Property taxes," he says. "House was worth too much. My daddy's. Had to let them take it, or it would have been an extra five years in Renewal."

"How long was it?" I say.

"Doesn't matter." He sucks his teeth. "Renewal doesn't leave time for real work. Lost everything else, too. Job, car, wife. Momma lived long enough in the home to hear about them taking the house."

"Jesus," I say. In graduate school, I couldn't work a real job either. Class schedules and homework loads and teaching duties kept me beholden to student loans for survival.

He nods. "Turns out, I'm damn good at it though. Got me this job after long enough. You learn things in here, Cade."

I wonder what else is behind that locked door.

He pours me another drink. "You learn to be careful."

I lift the glass, and he catches my gaze. Sets his jaw. I can no longer read his expression. He holds it for a good while until he's convinced I've got it.

"Best you get to work," he says. There are only three hours left in my shift.

I swallow the drink, and my eyes swim. "Yes, sir."

He nods. "You're my first repossession, you know that?"

"No, sir."

"People can't really call you Dr. Cade anymore, can they?" he says.

"No, sir."

He gives me another good stare. Leans into it.

"Don't forget your sunblock."

It's regulation.

CHAPTER EIGHT

THIS TIME, I'M SHAKING. IT IS A SIDE EFFECT OF THE chemicals Cynthia is delivering into my bloodstream via the therapeutic sofa's intravenous lines.

"It happens sometimes."

She has applied a cold compress to my forehead above the goggles. Darkened the tint on the lenses. She runs her fingernails through my hairline, delicately, professionally. This is to source a feeling of safety, of comfort. The presence of others during times of duress engenders serenity among the afflicted. Most of our waking efforts, our genetic imperatives, involve the struggle against isolation. Consciousness is largely a social process, despite what we tell ourselves about personal landscapes and the mysterious interiority of our come-and-go selves.

What she is doing is sterile. Medicinal. We have known this since women first clutched butchered men to their breasts in our greatest wars. Since men learned to stay with each other as they died. To lay on hands. Solitude is only a means of better seeking company.

She says soft things while I convulse on these cushions. The room is filled with her perfume. Hypersensitivity is another problem of this process—hence the goggles. They restrict stimuli in soothing, dark ways.

"Are—we accomplishing anything?" I say. Barely.

"Hush, Ben."

"But we're not—talking."

"You'll be better soon."

This time, I do not float. There is no wine-dark sea. I weigh like Tungsten. A neutron star. The world is drawn across geometric arcs and probabilities, to me. We're fixing what I know—too much—by bringing me everything else. I am a singularity, an event horizon, a form of myself beyond the confines of my brain. Beyond spherical time and distance—the light in this room will never escape the pull of my mind.

The sofa makes meditative sounds, long mechanical vowels. The voice of God, formless upon the water. I have some shape— God's own image—I am a self in other realities. The convergence of all things—every life at once. Sometimes, the only difference between dimensions is the particular motion of something tiny— electrons, neutrinos, and the quarks of higher consciousness. I am.

That's all it takes—one blip, one influence from something you can't control. Like Brownian motion, or beta decay, or losing your job. Somewhere, something falls apart invisibly—an electron breaking rules—and a new reality is born. They all exist, every possibility in every instance. In some other life, I have darker skin. Somewhere, I am alone. Somewhere, I am the one doing this to Cynthia.

It happens here—the center of the galaxy on this sofa, buzzing, buzzing.

I try to hum with the sofa. The room is so thick through these goggles.

"Are we—accomplishing anything?"

Somewhere, I exist. A different me, sourced here, outside the confines of normal time. I still remember parts of the theory, but not its name. It will collapse entirely. A black hole I can't even see— that never existed—by the time Cynthia is finished.

I remember talking about it with someone, somewhere. It's a figure from a dream: several people at once, and we talked in places that were not what they were. That changed every continuing instant, until I woke up. Sometime. It might have been Sireen. I can't remember which theories she likes and which make her uncomfortable.

Field Methodology was almost as hard as Syntax. He set us loose on a language we didn't know.

Figure it out, my director said to us. That's the point.

Sign language. He'd hired a deaf man to sign. About anything he wanted to. And we had to break his code. Turn him from a cipher into a human. We'd been warned that, now and then, there had been FBI in these classes. Clandestine students on the long con, looking for the next crack troupe of cryptographers. Even if they didn't even know it yet. I knew people who were approached. Some went on to help organize Renewal.

How did the old woman get her husband into bed? my director said, to break the classroom tension. Some loaded joke I wouldn't understand until later.

She   a   -   when he   '   .

"Yes, Ben," Cynthia says. "We're accomplishing things."

He was the only one who could laugh.

Cynthia hums with me, her enameled nails like chips of red earth. The dust at the beginning of time.

She finally administers a sedative. She has been pinching the line between the fingers of her off-hand, waiting. Counting minutes like days. All things in time.

Now we may begin. Let there be light.

○

The piece of paper, which Cynthia advised me to give to Sireen, once I got home, claims that I may be experiencing *flattening of affect* as a side effect of today's session. That seems to mean that I'll lack emotional reactivity. Cynthia suggests that Sireen give me some painkillers and a sleep aid, if I become confused or disoriented.

I feel fine. Just a little uninterested. I'm not big into emotion in the first place. I don't think anyone still is. It's certainly not worth it.

I think about something else. About air and buildings, things immediately around me while walking the safe, sun-filled alleys back toward our house.

"Space" is important. I have to remember. It is simply what it is—area, possibility. The potential for things to be. Space has no meaning.

"Place" has meaning. It is human psychology. Sociology. The projection of importance onto meaningless things. Even an empty building—like these old storefronts—is a place.

It's a big part of understanding "meaning." Being. I think.

Space is important because spaces imply things—like organisms. For example, even though nothing lives on the moon, it still implies an organism. The organism it implies does not require water, is impervious to ultraviolet radiation, and has no use for air. It doesn't exist, but if it did.

This city block implies only that structures adhere to the laws of gravity and eventual decay.

But space also implies what you can do with it, to it. The nature of what you can do to or with a thing is an *affordance*. I remember.

This empty sidewalk before these empty storefronts implies that two men can attack another one because there is ample room for it. There are two men demonstrating this across the street. I'm waiting beneath a fire escape until they are done. It seems the best reaction.

The sidewalk implies that the man with the coffee cup and the candy bar can smash his face into its pavement when his attackers knock him down. Which he does. It implies that he may bleed upon it.

They don't take his wallet. What's the point anymore? One attacker picks up the candy bar where it fell. Candy bars afford dropping. He runs away. The other attacker bends over the discarded coffee cup, lifts it, sees that too little coffee remains inside, and demonstrates that paper cups afford crushing. He walks away.

This is how it all works. So I wait a few minutes before emerging. The downed man is not in my way, which affords my avoidance of him. I can't imagine how hot the pavement must be on his skin. Gray-white-hot, like the surface of the moon. Which burns a different way. Doubtless, even the moon implies muggings, should you live there.

This is how we understand our place in the universe. The real one. The meaning of life.

I feel fine. I have my hand in my pocket. The note to Sireen folded safely under my fingers.

I'll need a new safe route home.

○

I wait to meet Zoe near the alley where she turned in her introductory essay—her performance art proposal. The heat is dry, which is odd. It rains often here. Our valley traps vehicle exhaust and industrial pollutants. It revisits them upon us in ozone alerts and acid rain.

Sireen and I don't go out in the heat. What it does to the skin isolates us. We forget the other of us in our discomfort, reduced from our higher selves. A "flattening of affect," I guess. I looked it up. It used to happen to schizophrenics.

Zoe has invited me for lunch.

I don't remember which of these bricked spaces she chose for her performance-art essay, so I don't bother searching. It's enough to stand near this block of newspaper bins and pretend to read *The Mountainist*. It's counter-cultural, hip—something to keep the intelligent young busy.

The feature article is about adults who are facing eviction or foreclosure. Most of them take to the streets or join tent cities. The socially forward—who once ate tofu and flax seed in their expensive homes, who thought they understood free trade, who dislike chemicals—are different. They've begun offering themselves up for adoption by other families, where they will perform domestic services for their new family. The taxable heads of these households, in addition to a sense of entitled philanthropy, the article explains, are eligible for additional tax deductions because the adoptees become dependents.

Some of the hopeful have even taken to creating handbills and online profiles that infantilize them. A few are posted in *The Mountainist* itself. In the back, where the escort services and beauty products are advertised.

"Dr. Cade!" Zoe says. She is carrying a motorcycle helmet under her arm, jogging through the sun. I can understand why she wears only a bikini top and cut-off shorts.

The number of host families is increasing, I read quickly.

"Dr. Cade—"

"Ben. Please."

Technically, I am no longer a doctor. I am now lacking the full completion of my final credit hours, since Cynthia has repossessed what I learned during my last semester. At the conclusion of our last session, I signed the affidavit that surrenders my rights of ownership of my dissertation. My alma mater will be forced to surrender them as well. It's the law.

Zoe shifts her helmet to her other arm and squints into the sun, as if trying to find me there. Which would be absurd. The sun affords very little, while also affording everything.

"Ben," she says. "Let's eat."

○

They look at me in here. Blank, sweating. There are fans pulling the dead air through repurposed industrial windows. There is no air conditioning. Most homes and small businesses in this city don't use it. The temperature is usually too mild, and most remaining a/c units don't work anyway.

"What is this, Zoe?" It looks like a soup kitchen.

She lays a palm on my shoulder—the undershirt I'm wearing—as she moves past, already sourcing handshakes from half a dozen of these people. She has the moves that make them happen.

She's doing something to her consciousness. Pushing it. Something.

"Come on, Dr. Cade."

I'm realizing that they're only looking at me because of how attention works. I think. Attention is consciousness, which requires a certain minimum time period of steady neuronal stimulation. It's not very long, but it's long enough. I can't remember.

And, really, it was probably Zoe's cleavage that drew their eyes this way.

Beyond the thirty or so people, against a white cinder block wall, cans of gelatinized fuel burn on top of a folding table lined with chafing dishes. Some things are warm. There are also sandwiches. Fruit.

Zoe puts her arm around my shoulders.

"It's all local," she says. "The building is co-op owned."

"That's good," I say.

I see David, Zoe's friend from class, behind the table—he looks proud, glad that I'm here to share his progressive enthusiasm. He wears the clothes. The hair. I don't really care.

"David," I say. "Good to see you."

"You too, Dr. Cade," he says. He smiles at Zoe. "Hey."

"What would you like?" Zoe says to me.

"Nothing for me. Thanks." I smile for her, too. "I don't have . . . I didn't bring any money."

She pulls a stack of bill-sized papers from her crocheted handbag. They look like toy money. Something from a grocery store. From years ago, when they sold toys like essentials.

Zoe peels a few off the stack and hands them to David. He tucks them into stacks of other bills inside a cash box. He looks like he's trying to pay attention to anything but her.

"Get whatever you like," she says.

○

"How does it work?"

Zoe hands me one of the bills. I examine it with my off-hand. I am using the other to eat a blemished apple. The placard in front of the basket of apples informed me that these were grown within my zip code. "Nothing but sun and rain." Which is good. The radon gas trapped in all these hills is going to kill us anyway. No sense hurrying it with bad food or chemical fertilizers.

The bill is done up in black and red ink. A sort of mid-century modern design block. It says 1 SHARE in impressive, hip letters. I could use it in class, teaching visual rhetoric. It follows all the rules.

"Same principle as regular cash," she says.

"You're printing your own money?"

"Does that bother you?"

She likes this. Whether she intended to or not, she . . . arranged, or whatever, this conversation according to her self-satisfaction with things like free education, dreadlocks, riding motorcycles, and flaunting her skin. Certainly, she has to be abrasive about these things with her peers—establishing order, rank, genuine interest. Not with me. She wants me to be impressed with her street-wise expertise. She wants validation, of the things she thinks.

More importantly, though, she's compensating, acting authoritative, even (especially) around David. But for what, who the fuck knows.

I put my apple down. "Not really."

She stabs at a bowlful of greens. "These people can't get jobs, but they have things to offer. Skills, labor hours, apples. You sign up with the SHARE committee, record a number of volunteer hours, or produce donations, or whatever you have, and then the committee hands you a stack of bills."

"Are you on the committee?"

"No. The office is upstairs, though. We could meet some, I'll bet."

"How does the committee fund itself?"

"It takes dues from those who buy in and sells what it can."

"I see."

There is a small piercing hole in her cheek, near her nose, where she must sometimes wear a stud. I can see that now.

"Where do you spend them?" I say.

"There's a registry," she says, "of participants. People, establishments. You can trade labor for more SHARES, or you can spend them on produce, handcrafts—whatever."

"Clever," I say. Until the committee gets out of hand.

"It's all underground," she says. I'm sure she likes that part. "Un-taxed."

Un-taxed. Despite the committee's dues. It's important to own one's language. The usage and meaning of it, for things like this.

"Do you want me to sign you up?" she says.

I give her a look, like I'm thinking. "Why are you taking my class, Zoe? Are you learning anything?"

One shouldn't ask two questions in a row, rhetorically speaking. It yields the initiative when sourcing subject-object discourse relationships. I know better. It feels weird to know better.

She points at the copy of *The Mountainist* that I carried in with me.

"Did you like the article?" she says.

"It's disturbing."

"Did you think it was well-written?"

"Well enough. The journalist could use some practice."

"That's why." She's not posturing when she smiles now. The dead air blows between us.

"You want to write articles," I say.

"Something like that," she says.

"Yes, then," I say.

"Yes, what?"

"Yes, I want you to sign me up."

○

Outside, a kid walks past wearing a pair of chimping goggles. They are plugged into his mobile phone via a cord and a small adapter.

"They use wireless phone signals now," Zoe tells me. "To network. It's all mobile."

"I see."

CHAPTER NINE

THERE ARE TWO POLICEMEN WAITING AT THE TOP OF THE amphitheater stairs in Sentinel Park. My students wait quietly, in rank and file, on the stone terraces beneath them. There are around sixty of them. By this point, it has become clear which ones are friends. Which ones are dating. Who thinks he's smarter than the others. The retirees are the most diligent.

For many of them, this class is the characterization of their entire lives. Their frustration. Their underground madness. Like me, most of these have been conditioned against neurological imbalance since childhood—standing in line outside the school nurse's office, waiting for their vaccinations and their turns with the adhesive pads that warmed their brains against madness. This is as close as they can come to being disturbed. Doing things that agitate their better sense.

This or a pair of chimping goggles.

"Benjamin Cade?" one of the officers says. The other stares at the students, at the traffic in the surrounding thoroughfares. Anything.

"Yes."

He looks about my age. He is armed with a sidearm, a taser, a telescopic billy club, and several canisters of chemical irritant.

Police officers often do not go to post-graduate school. Some departments no longer even require a bachelor's degree, because it is unfeasible, considering their hiring needs. I read an article that explained as much.

"I need to ask you about your relationship with Leah Johnson," the officer says.

Declarative intent is not a question. It is insidious. It establishes a position of subject authority. It performs the task of making demands without making them. I can cooperate, if I like.

"Very well."

He frowns. "*Do* you have a relationship with Miss Johnson?"

"I may," I say. "Who is she?"

I look into the amphitheater, plumbing depth and attendance from on high, with these officers.

The officer shows me a photograph of Zoe. It is a candid shot: she is descending the stoop in front of an apartment building—somewhere downtown, judging by the ashlars and stringcourses in the architecture. She is not looking at the photographer. There are handwritten numbers along the bottom.

I think about the woman on the chimping network.

"This person attends my class," I say. "On occasion."

I see David in the crosswalk across the street, coming late to class. When he sees the officers, he paints them with his best hatred gaze and reverses his direction.

"Where can we find her?"

I wonder if he means *we* in the sense of law enforcement collectively, or if he is actualizing semantic cooperation. A game to determine who I am and what I will do.

I turn away and stare again into the amphitheater. "She doesn't seem to be here today."

He wants me to ask him if there's a problem. If Zoe's in some kind of trouble. Play along.

But I couldn't care less. Zoe is interesting because she is interesting, not because I feel attached. One must keep distances between oneself and one's students. One should, anyway.

He hands me his business card. I put it in my pocket without looking at it.

"If you see her again," he says, "let her know that we'd like to ask her a few questions."

"Will there be anything else, officer?"

"Yes. Class is canceled. City ordinance."

"Which ordinance is that?"

"If you are caught fomenting civic discord in public again, you will be detained."

"It's a *rhetoric* class."

The quiet one produces a copy of *The Mountainist*. The first officer opens it to the page containing my original advertisement for the class. He points to the chimpanzee image I used.

"Are you associated with any groups that identify with this imagery, Mr. Cade?"

"It's just an advertisement," I say. "Chimpanzees seem to be the thing these days. I thought it would attract people to my class."

"This group has become an organization of interest," he says. "I recommend that you don't reference their imagery again."

He hands the circular back to his partner. "Have a nice evening, Mr. Cade."

○

"That's it," I say.

I can't figure out if I'm angry or not. It was bound to happen, and sooner or later, I wouldn't even be capable of teaching it anymore anyway. I don't know how I was going to end it.

Most of them just stand up and go. Move along.

I never cared when students dropped my class. It made my job easier.

"What do we do now?" one says. One of the retirees.

"I don't know," I say. "Teach each other. Keep it up."

"Good luck, Dr. Cade."

"Thanks," I say. They're being emotional. Standing there in a little group. Staring at me for some parting experience. Something to cap it all off while the classmates they smiled at and chatted with and waved to in happy coincidences in the bread line, exchanging quips about missed classes and their plans for the weekend. While those classmates become inert humanshapes around them. Irrelevant to experience.

I watch the dispersal.

"Et cetera," I say.

⬡

"لا، حالته سيئة كتير." Sireen says. She's talking into her phone, in her palm, where her mother's face tries to remain steady upon the screen. Her tremors are only getting worse. The video image brings them into Sireen's life every few weeks, when they talk. They never speak of it—the disease. But I see Sireen's efforts, from time to time, on her computer. The files and sites and browsing odysseys that take her into her mother's world, where she tries to understand dying. And I can tell when she's talking to her cousin. The doctor in Beirut. Who answers idiot questions and dispenses reassurance and yes he'll talk to his colleagues at the hospital. Only the best. Everything we can do.

"لا، ابدا ما حيرضا." Sireen says.

I only met her mother once, at our wedding. It was in the middle of a semester because the venue was cheaper then. We paid for it with our student loan disbursement. Her mother stayed with us that weekend. I had a paper to write.

Sireen waves at me. I stop in the middle of the living room. Just stand there.

"لا، عندي زملاء بيئدرو. بتوع كمبيوتر. هن بيعرفو." Sireen says.

It was in the   . Little cups of Turkish coffee that I'd fucked up, but Huda, her mother, was too nice   . She smiled almost as much as Sireen did, who was out at   .

It's okay, Ben, حبيبي, she said. You'll do everything. Write your paper. What is it about?

‑   .   ,

·

"... ايوة. انا بدبر كل شي." Sireen points the screen at me, and extends her arm.

"Hello, Ben, حبيبي," Huda says.

I lift a hand and wave. "Hello, Huda."

She loves you, Huda said. She'll do everything. Just like you.

She lived the civil war, back in Lebanon. Was still steely with it. Still looking at everything like a revolution. Including us.

"باي ماما." Sireen says.

Especially us.

Sireen goes over to see her sometimes, a few weeks in the summer. She hasn't mentioned it in a few months.

She ends the call.

"They canceled the class," I say.

"What?" Sireen says. "Who canceled it?"

She sets down her phone, tucks her legs underneath her on the couch. There is a glass of wine on the floor beneath her. She is still wearing the nylons she worked in today.

"The police."

"What?" She moves a pile of rosters and homework assignments from one cushion to another. Making room for the conversation. For me.

"They were just looking for one of the students," I say.

"Are you in trouble?" she says. I can't tell if she's angry or afraid.

"No."

She looks down at her wine. "Shit. I'm sorry."

We didn't get the bungalow we liked. One of the other tourists outbid us.

"I'm going for a drink," I say. "You want one?"

"I can't," she says. Hefts the papers to demonstrate.

"Okay."

○

There is a sign on the door. My neighborhood bar now accepts SHARES. That changes things. I walk inside quickly, and I can see through the other door that most of the patrons are on the large patio in the back, drinking and flirting under out-of-season Christmas lights and neon beer signs. They wear layered clothing in casual, ironic ways, despite the heat.

The bartender recognizes me.

"Gin martini," I say. "Whatever's in your well."

She turns around.

"And a pair of goggles," I say.

I start picking SHAREs out of the stack the committee gave me when Zoe signed me up. Back pay, they called it. For all I was doing for the community as a teacher. I took them—all two hundred. I don't care. I can order a decent drink now.

I walk to a booth. The bartender can bring the drink to me.

○

I enjoy feeling like I'm in control. I don't know what this sim is, what I'm experiencing. I didn't even bother reading the title from the menu. The goggles' microchip selected it at random from the list of simulations that have been approved and licensed for public use. The subscriber fees for the simulations with restricted licenses, those for use only in private theaters, are too high to pay.

Even if you could pay, and you hacked the appropriate servers, databases—whatever—if you altered the registry for your goggles you'd be arrested if you were caught chimping restricted sims in public places. Disorderly conduct against the common good.

The sim takes the edge off. Things feel a little better. It is making me micromanage my impulses. Choosing, selecting, directing the stream of my own consciousness. At least, that's how it feels. If I had to guess, I'd say that the neuronal processes generating my sense of self are being regrouped in some scalar fashion, higher-order to lower, that creates the illusion of associative control. A feeling of control is just the dump and slosh of communicative neuro-chemicals anyway. I remember that much.

What had kept Zoe from class? She never skipped. And David, going to ground when he saw the cops across the street. I didn't bother noticing who else wasn't in class. Who else knew not to show up. I should have paid attention. I can't figure out if I'm angry or not. If I would have been once.

Emotion is just auto-correction, I tell myself. My self tells me—the sim reclaiming control. It's the brain qualifying whatever experience for proper storage. Having names for emotions, like anger—and figuring out how to create them with goggles made of cheap plastic and electrodes manufactured in plants overseas—those are the consequences of being both a psychological *and* a sociological being. The sim in action. We exist *out there*, beyond ourselves, whether we like it or not. Behavior must be named and moderated by the masses. We feel what the outside world has best taught us to feel. To keep things in line.

The martini helps.

The goggles superimpose a network connection request icon in my field of vision.

No one is sitting particularly near to me; I can talk to myself all I want.

I approve the request.

"You're back," she says, "Ben." Her voice, like the first time, is digitally altered.

The last time I chimped, when Sireen and Dimitri and I played "Jim and Carol," I didn't tell them that Jim, the associative identity that had been fully indexed and processed and offered up to the simulation for the sake of whatever behavioral research his debtors sold him to, and then again to the company manufacturing and distributing consumer-grade goggles and simulations—I hadn't told them that, in love though he was, he was afraid of what would become of him and Carol. He had doubts. I had them for him. We are more than our simulated selves, real or otherwise, but it sure didn't fucking feel that way.

Sireen and I had sex that night. All the liquor. The goggles. That simulation. It scared me, though it shouldn't have. I'm not Jim.

I didn't want to talk about it.

I adjust the goggles' microphone. "I'm back," I say.

"Did you miss me?" she says.

"Fuck you."

"I'm feeling submissive tonight."

"You should."

"Don't flatter yourself," she says. "It's the sim."

"It's all the same to me," I say. "You might as well be a sim yourself."

She makes a little noise.

"Your name isn't Carol, is it?" I say.

"Do you want to know my name?"

"Isn't that supposed to be a secret?"

"I'll tell you."

"And I'm supposed to believe you?"

"Please," she says. "I'll tell you the truth."

The dial for the intensity of the simulation is on the opposite earpiece from the one housing the broadcast button. I thumb it up a couple of degrees. I'm enjoying this. It enjoys me.

"What do you want?" I say.

"Do you want to meet me someplace? Private?"

I change my mind and dial the sim back down. I don't know what this woman is on, but all I can think about is being arrested. I have no idea how far you can go on public channels like this.

The coincidence makes me nervous. I randomly selected something dominant, and tonight she's being submissive. I don't like it.

"I'm married," I say. "Jesus."

"I know."

Jesus.

"What do you mean, you know?"

She makes a little noise. I'm feeling pressure behind my eyes. In my fingertips. She's making me angry.

"Answer me!"

I feel a thousand tiny fists along the top of my skull, down my spine. I close my eyes against the warmth, the vertigo. Breathe deeply.

I want to shout again.

"People know who you are," she says. "You teach downtown."

"Jesus. How do you know that?"

"I told you not to use your real name. People find things."

"Yeah, thanks for the fucking tip."

"So, what's new?" she says.

"You want to *chat*?"

"That's the point, Ben," she says. "It's not as fun alone."

It takes great effort not to lash out at her again. To call her a cunt and threaten to find her, on the other end, and teach her a lesson.

Which must be the point of this sim.

Jesus.

I swallow some martini. "You know I teach. Well, class has been canceled."

"It's getting too big. You're making a scene."

I think about it. There had only been a dozen or so of them on the first day of class. Now, weeks later, there are between sixty and a hundred, depending on what else is going on around town that night. It is a place to be seen, so people watch. I don't bother learning their names.

"Maybe."

Maybe it's gotten too big for itself. It became its own sociological entity, so it was subject to the same entropic breakdown of its constituent parts as anything else. Organizations, marriages, educations.

Which would have made me the figurehead. Godhead. The end of all things as far as class was concerned. Their behavior was mine. I used to study the psychogeographical effects of one's surroundings on one's consciousness. On the emotions it creates to keep the world in line. Space itself.

"There's no maybe about it. You caught the wrong attention," she says.

She's parroting my thoughts. It's making me angry.

The martini helps.

"I don't think you even know, Ben. They formed study groups."

"What?"

She doesn't sound submissive anymore. I think she's dialed down her intensity.

"Your class pets ran them, in their apartments and in community centers and in civic clearspace with bottles of cheap beer."

"Jesus."

"Miss Johnson ran one. So did David Forrester."

"Wait." This is running together. You can't dial the intensity to zero without canceling the sim. I'm losing control, and it's making my hands shake.

"Why study groups? It was fucking introductory rhetoric. Composition. A little philosophy sometimes."

"You were hard to understand, and getting harder. Not all of your lessons were complete."

"Were you a student?"

"Don't worry, Ben. The class will go on."

"The fuck it will! I'm not getting fucking arrested for a bunch of unemployed kids in a city park. I have a wife! We're buying a fucking house!"

I get a little warmer. Shake a little less. The bartender gives me an eye from across the room. *Calm the fuck down, sir.*

"It will be secure this time," she says. "Not just a place to be seen. You'll be driven there."

"And you're going to what, bus all my students to this place?"

"Some of them. The good ones."

Admissions criteria. Restricted enrollment. The same old shit.

"You're defeating the fucking point, whoever the fuck you are. Sounds like elitist horseshit to me."

"You know who I am."

"Who are you?"

"Use your fucking brain, Ben."

○

Sireen and I attend a grocery auction. One of her colleagues told her about it. Someone for whom the professorial salary isn't enough. Someone with kids to feed, two car payments, and old medical expenses. Something.

I hate grocery shopping. The people, the carts, the bovine suppression of awareness. Everybody's alone at the grocery store, getting in each other's ways. But I go with Sireen. She likes to take her time, selecting vegetables, inspecting cans. I try to say as little as possible while we're there. I carry the reusable bags. We used to shop with actual baskets, at an organic co-op down the road from her apartment, and I would select obscure beers while Sireen sampled the oils and hand lotions. The hand-knit scarves she tied around her throat in the fall. She laughed at the workers' jokes, and meant it.

Sireen's colleague told her that most of the groceries at the auction are legal—surplus or near-expiration. There are a few pallets of produce from local farmers, for whom the shrinking federal subsidies aren't enough. They farm to keep busy. Raising food that can't pay for itself, for inflation. I imagine they haven't heard yet about SHARES.

Some of the goods are stolen, by teamsters, inventory managers, petty thugs.

I park our sedan in the community center parking lot. There are very few empty spaces. The auction takes place on the basketball court, inside.

○

We hold hands as we browse the impromptu aisles. There are cabbages and damaged canned goods and packages of toilet paper with defective labels. There are colorful ziggurats of vitamins and supplements, the products of a buy-in, sell-yourself pyramid scheme I looked into a few months ago. They call it multi-level marketing. The farmers and vendors and wholesale representatives stand against the walls, talking in cross-armed groups. They drink coffee from Styrofoam cups and watch us askance. Like parents, waiting for something in this gymnasium to cheer about. Like the dispossessed adults in *The Mountainist*, looking for adoption, who would gladly play basketball for these people.

The aisles are not tall—a foot or two, at most. Sireen points out lot numbers, and I jot them down on a legal pad she took from her department's supply closet. As attendees, we're given an hour to inspect the lots before we must take our seats in the bleachers.

When we sit, thigh-to-thigh with our neighboring strangers, I hold Sireen's purse so she can unfold the tabs on our bidding paddle. It folds in on itself and tucks into place. Many people are using them as fans.

Sireen listens to the auctioneer, glancing at our list of lot numbers. Waiting.

"So," I say, "I heard something about the class."

"Yeah?" she says, arching one eyebrow. Performing attention even though she isn't paying it. She watches her list.

Someone bids fiercely on a crate of expired saltine crackers.

"They formed study groups. Before it was canceled."

Sireen laughs. Then she looks up quickly—exaggeratedly interested, to cover the slip.

"That's great," she says. "They must really have been interested."

I watch one of the farmers drag his tomatoes front and center with a hand truck. It's his turn. I'm still holding Sireen's purse.

"Maybe they still get together," I say.

She purses her lips. Looks at her ledger. "We're next."

"Apparently, some of my lectures were hard to understand."

She laughs for real this time. Gets a hand on my knee, as if she's reaching for balance.

○

We have to balance our goods in teetering stacks in the parking lot. Some of the other people came prepared. They have dollies and repurposed luggage wheelers outfitted with plastic crates and bungee cords. We are careful, moving with the exodus toward our car.

Sireen says something about the savings. About the auction next week. There are two men arguing over a box of produce five parking spaces over from ours. Each of them has his fingers laced through the ventilation holes in the box. The trunk of the mini-van behind them lights their foreheads.

I let Sireen arrange our things. I hand them to her and watch the argument. People are ignoring the men, even in the adjacent spaces.

"Ben," Sireen says, capturing my attention.

I turn to look. Behind me, gunshots erupt. Loud ones. A handgun with a short muzzle—a revolver, maybe. Sireen squats, her hands upon her ears. I see her pivot on the balls of her feet—left, right. She's unsure what to do. People are screaming. Footfalls slapping. I feel the thundering herd against my shoulders. Fear is one of our most primary emotions. It is the clash of reflex, instinct, muscle memory against the social self. Which is the hesitation to ignore one's better sense, one's sleeping self, because this is civilization after all. There are no predators in the savannah grass here. Nothing to be afraid of.

There is only one man behind the mini-van now. The trunk canopies him. The interior light now reveals very little. He is on the pavement. His fingers still grasp the overturned box. Its lid is sealed with packing tape. There are more shots, not far away. Screaming.

I feel that pressure behind my eyes. Like the simulation. Those fists upon my spine. The urge, the dominant impulse that the goggles have taught me to resist. To crave. I want to give in. Do what a man should do. I am a pump—fear and light and instinct trapped by the valves in my bloodstream.

"Ben!"

I want to open those valves—to destroy them with some adrenal blast. I want to release the tide and watch it rain for forty days.

"Ben! Please!"

I allow my sense of self to rearrange itself, from higher- to lower-scalar orders. It creates the illusion of control. So I can do what a man does. Despite my immediate fear.

I run. Through the jostling crowd. There are people standing around the victim. Staring. Some at the box of produce. He isn't moving. I dig my fingers into his neck, but I can't tell. His pulse or mine? There's nothing about him doing any of the things that look like living. What are the clues? I can't remember. My pants sponge his blood where my knees touch the pavement. I'm not in control here. My bloodstream is moving things along in pressurized bursts. Clenching and sealing and flowing away. I am only the flotsam of my fluid self.

Other people are touching him now, too. Laying on hands, and palming blood, and being part of the process. None of us are good at it.

Someone grabs the box of produce. He isn't one of us, down here, being together in the blood. He doesn't get very far before I bloodstream him to the ground and face face face against the concrete. I'm only good enough at it. Because it is difficult to grasp his head with so much blood between my fingers.

Sireen's sudden hands are cool on my neck. Hard and deep into my windpipe, and we're halfway back to the car, and I'm surprised. She makes me set down the dead man's box of produce. I dumbgrabbed it, getting up. Maybe. I don't know. Someone else carries it immediately away.

There is a traffic jam, exiting the parking lot. Sireen drives.

CHAPTER TEN

TODAY, I HAVE BEEN INSTRUCTED TO WEAR PLAIN CLOTHES during my Renewal shift. Rosie moved me up in the monitor rotation, but he wouldn't explain why. I'm not sure if he despises me or thinks I'm okay.

He hands me a mobile phone. It is more advanced than the one I own, and it has a serial number stenciled along the back. The artist was careful to avoid the camera lenses.

"You're only responsible for two efficiency observations, since it's your first time," Rosie says. "Disorderly conduct counts."

"Where do I have to do this?" I say.

He hands me a printout of some city streets that are within feasible walking distance of downtown—so it won't look strange that I'm on them. One of the streets is zoned commercial.

"Don't tell anyone what you're doing," he says. "Be discreet when you're ready to send me what you see. Find someplace out of the way."

I study the map. The header states that I am not allowed to remove it from my dispatcher's office. It contains digital signatures from the Senate Efficiency Committee under the motto that "Efficiency is everyone's responsibility."

I hand it back to him, and I stand there. He's watching me. He just waves the map away, so I fold it into my pocket.

"I don't want to do this," I say.

"I know."

"You know they canceled my class," I say. "The one I was teaching for free downtown."

He sucks on the bridge in his teeth.

"Yeah."

"Was there a monitor in that class?" I say.

"Of course there was."

The day-by-day calendar on his desk is two weeks out of date. I could report him. He isn't using state resources correctly.

"Jesus, Rosie," I say. "I was helping people."

He looks. Outside, someone coughs. Waiting to check in.

"You are one dumb motherfucker," he says. "You think I had a choice?"

I decide it's better not to ask why the cops are after Zoe.

◌

Being a monitor turns me into a tourist. I walk my own city's streets in search of things to notice, to remember. I look for evidence that I am someplace more interesting, more dangerous, more romantic than my home. I listen for other languages and expressions, so I can be sure this trip was worth it. I take photographs of simple things in foreign circumstances.

This turns us all into strangers. I can't know anyone. Their lives and answers. I have to see them as a monitor because they are threats to themselves.

I did this once in Paris, before, when Sireen and I had a little money, and Central was paying for her ticket so she could give a lecture. I wandered the streets around the Sorbonne, looking for things to look at. Mostly, I smoked cigarettes and tried to hide from the winter air. I tried to get lost, but I just ended up at the Eiffel Tower. Sireen met me there, after her talk, and we climbed the steps in the freezing evening rain.

The lights were large and dispassionate. They strobed, in their thousands, to make the tower glitter for tourists in the distance. I'd forgotten about them. The guidebook said they were not to be missed. A holdover from an installation as old as the new millennium.

91

Jesus, Sireen said. They're fucking bright. She was doing all the talking. I only knew enough French to buy cigarettes and croissants. And only sort of. They couldn't tell the difference between my *de* and *deux*. The air warmed, close to the lights. I pulled us there, and she squealed. Her teeth were cold when I pressed my lips into her smile. We squinted against the rain and the light.

It's Romantic, she said. Being bright and cold. Really makes you pay attention.

The next day, climbing the stairs from the riverwalk along the bank of the Seine, we became accidentally trapped between protesting students and the police force's shield wall. Sireen nearly caught a billy club to the head, but one of the cops figured us out in time. I jogged us away, past the gathered *gendarmerie*, so helpfully labeled by the stencils on their raincoats, and they weren't interested except in their submachine guns and who was taking pictures of the conflict.

I wanted the students to win.

Where are we going? Sireen said. I dragged her into   plaza, a little urban hollow of lichened marble and oxidized brass fencing. They built it to commemorate   his   contributions   to   -
            -          , which was just a casual reality over here.

                              , I said.

This is how I loved her.

○

This block contains mostly apartment buildings. I see chimpanzee stencils on two different walls in two different alleyways. I try to look like I belong, which is what we do in foreign territory.

○

This apartment is empty. The door handle had a realtor's lock box on it, but both the box and the front door were unlocked. One of the other tenants saw me walking down the hall. She turned her head quickly because I indicate bad things to her, by not looking away first.

There is nothing in the apartment. Even the doors to some of the cupboards are missing. The light fixtures, the copper tubing under the sink. Its living room windows face the street, so I sit cross-legged in front of one. I place Rosie's phone within reach.

I see only the city. It feels meditative. Almost religious. As if I'm supposed to divine meaning from the patterns of sunlight or the routes of wandering pedestrians. Civic haruspex—learning secrets by looking into our municipal entrails.

There is a mail center across the street, on the bottom floor of the apartment building facing this one. Its neon sign says OPEN, but no one moves behind the window. Above it, there is the play of shadow from the pecan trees outgrowing their cleared spaces in the sidewalk concrete. There are stone stringcourses and ornamental water spouts on some floors. There is laundry hanging from small balconies, still in the day.

If I could move through these walls, then this would be easier. This job I don't want. I could move between planes of sheet rock, decaying insulation, fiberglass grit. I could move like a miner, underground, inhaling small things that are too sharp for my lungs, things that glitter in the dark air, as if there is something there. If I could stick my fingers through electrical outlets, I could take photographs of people doing things—using the toilet, or smoking pot, or fomenting revolution. At night, I could dust them with cleaning powders and chemical agents, between chapped night-lips or upon pulsing eyelids. I could correct things, chemically, like repossession in reverse. I could make them see with my fistfuls of black mold and rust. I might hear their evening prayers.

It's hot in here, like a sweat lodge. My feet begin to fall asleep, so I get up to pace. I become my own silence. A quiet mind. There is less of me in this apartment by the moment, and I create what I see. Perception is involved, somehow. I don't remember. It's not seeing things.

I know Dimitri does this type of thing. He and his colleagues sit in small rooms on research campuses and watch footage of people. They study behavior, isolation, the suspension of higher faculties. I know they keep records and make notes and send their graduate students for fresh trays of coffee. Meanwhile, people in rooms, like this one, watch TV or perform menial tasks or exhibit whatever specific behavior. He told me once about an inmate in solitary confinement he studied during grad school. The guy plucked out and ate his own eyeball after enough time in the small dark. Because it made sense, under the circumstances. He cooperated when Dimitri came in with three guards to record the color of his remaining eye. After all, he wasn't crazy. He'd been conditioned against it, just like the rest of us.

It is a particular instinct, that type of predatory observation. I didn't have to do it, earning my degrees. I simply read others' studies. I begin to become what I can see here, across the street. This apartment is my experimental chamber. It becomes all things. I become nothing but walls and floor tiles. An amnesiac resident. I have no past, no context. I am a monitor. Society itself. I become its breathing hallways, its empty spaces and windows. I become the man between the walls, like some ascetic in a holy space. Place. I become the woman across the way, cutting a man's hair in the light from the window. I become her neighbor, looking down, tugging at socks and damp floor towels as he prepares to shower. I become the singing silence of all these threatening images.

I eat my Renewal-issue sandwich and wonder about empty apartments. It is the spaces we must be concerned with because *people* don't originate their actions, threatening or otherwise—the contexts around them do. The brain initiates movement, action, cognition long before conscious awareness even gets involved. It's called readiness potential. I still remember. Cynthia hasn't gotten it yet. There are gaps, of hundreds of milliseconds, of non-being, when the brain gets going with the activities and ideas we think are *ours* before we even get a clue. *We* aren't in charge. The spaces around us, with their threats and opportunities and contextual stimuli are. They *react* the brain.

I am more than my defaulted loans. I am their consequences.

Meaning isn't an action in context, it's just context. We can't even properly perceive actions before we're doing something about them.

It is the spaces we must be concerned with. With clearing them out. Because of the contexts within them. With less context *reacting* us, we might all be safer. More efficient. I stare at the building across the road, and I wonder about its presence. Its residential spaces. Its malice.

○

I text Rosie.

Sorry. Nothing to report. Beginner's bad luck. Tack another day onto my record.

I leave my lunch trash on the floor as I stand to go.

Yes, you did, he texts. You saw a father teaching his son to play baseball, speaking Arabic. You saw people selling second-hand books without paying taxes on them.

I'm standing still. This conversation is having me.

What the fuck? Doesn't the government read these messages? This is fraud.

I am the government, Cade.

I didn't see those things.

Yes you did. It's better this way. Come turn in your phone.

I won't report Rosie either. It's better this way.

○

The heat wave broke like a blister. Last night, rain hammered between the mountain slopes that surround the city. It punched tiny holes in the smog that caps our valley, drawing fresh ozone like a chemical agent onto cracked leaves and aging roof shingles. It made things shine.

It's still raining this afternoon. I drag water from our flooded basement in five-gallon bucketfuls. The sump collects dirt down there, bugs. Odd metallic objects from previous tenants, because the pump is broken. I should feel honest, doing this work, but it pisses me off. We have fucking plumbing these days. Forget carrying essential things.

○

"Where are you going?" Sireen says.

She's watching an old movie. Black and white. She loves all of them—their shimmer and gleam. The poor resolution and lighting like paint. I usually watch with her because we take turns. She sits with me when I watch something she doesn't enjoy. Like documentaries about urban gangs or the World Wars. She sits close, where I can smell the almond oil she mixes into her lotion. When she gets bored, she starts to smile more. Sometimes she tries to put the lotion on my hands, because I hate it, to start something we can wrestle over.

"To teach," I say.

"In the rain? I thought class was canceled."

There's room for me on the couch. Her books on matrix mechanics, Algebraic K-theory, and differential topology are stacked neatly on the loveseat. She always leaves them where she's been. Or where I want to be.

I'm on—my books, she said. We'd started this in the kitchen. With a bottle of wine and a new album from one of her French bands.

Context is a bitch.

"You go to work in the rain," I say.

"Yes, but—"

That's sexy, I said. She had been studying in here earlier. The bedroom. There were hardback corners and unsteady sheets of paper against our wrists and necks. The comforter was dimpled where she'd lain, earlier.

Every conversation is fifty conversations at once.

"Don't worry," I say. "I won't let any cops see me teaching."

Every argument.

> It's uncomfortable, she said.
> You should recite—some formulae. From the books.
> Something exotic.

"Ben," she says—she's not smiling, "I wish you wouldn't."
Every damn thing at once.

> Not while—
> Try it, I said.
> $\Omega_n R^{n-1} \sinh^{n-1}$—she stopped. That's enough.

"Are you asking me to stay?" I say.
Fucking contexts. Like strata. Down in the dark. The good, the bad. The good, the bad. Everything is made of what it was before. Even this.

> Kinky.
> She pulled a book from under herself and halved it open behind my neck. She pulled it against my skin. Held on.

Especially this. She left me a note this morning, scheduling our next ovulation fuck. Listing her meetings for the day.
"No," she says. Looks away. "Do what you need to."

> Your turn, she said. But I didn't.

I don't need to go. I could stay. Fuck the students. I'm just delaying the inevitable.
But I've already upset her. What the hell. Before I'm even out the door, she's on the phone. In French. Which she saves for her old girlfriends.
"Tu étais supposé de me le faire savoir—"
On the front porch, I have no idea where I'm going. The text message I received yesterday, sent from some spoofed number, said only to go to the bus stop down the hill from our rental, near the halfway house. The wind blows my umbrella in all directions.

At the bus stop, under the canopy, I receive another text message: TEN MINUTES. The plexi-glassed schedule beside me reveals that no bus is due for another twenty.

There doesn't seem to be anyone watching me. No cops.

Eventually, Zoe drives up in a compact hybrid, and David gets out, folds down the front seat, and climbs into the back.

"Hello, Dr. Cade," Zoe says, inside. The car moves silently but for the hammering of the windshield wipers. Most of her dreads are concealed beneath an oversized black headband.

"Good evening," I say.

"Crazy, huh?" she says.

"This?"

"The rain."

○

The arts district doesn't seem very clandestine to me, but I don't complain. It exists along the rail line that cuts through town, down beside the river bottom beneath the commuter bridge. Most of the old depots and warehouses are studios now. Were studios. Ceramics, and sculpture, and oversized canvases. Dimitri brought me to show openings down here once or twice.

Now, they just look like derelict warehouses again.

Zoe drives between and around several. She pulls the car through a loading garage beneath a gantry tower.

"We're here."

There are work lights chained to the girders in the ceiling. They've been hooded with sheets of riveted tin, and they shine thirty feet down, between struts and pillars, to the circle of students. Twenty or thirty of them. They sit cross-legged on aged rugs and throw pillows. Someone has placed an easel in the center. With the oversized pad of newsprint I used in every class.

"Who set this up?" I say.

Zoe smiles at me.

"Answer me."

"We did, Dr. Cade," David says, behind me.

"All of you?"

98

"Everyone here. There." He points at the circle of students. The odor of cigarette smoke moves through the wet air. The rain is loud upon the corrugated steel lining the walls. It is dirty through the windows near the ceiling.

Someone lowers the overhead door behind us.

"And who are you all supposed to be?" I say.

"Come on," Zoe says.

There are two packs of hand-rolled cigarettes in repurposed packaging waiting for me upon the easel. A sandy-haired young man, Zoe's age, hands me a stack of SHAREs as he takes my jacket. He looks familiar. One of the other students passes a bottle to the girl beside her. It is unlabeled, a repurposed whisky bottle. Clear and heavy inside. I point at it as I push the lid off one of the markers on the easel.

○

"What exactly does 'meaning' mean?" I say.

Zoe tries. "Purpose?"

"No."

This group is young. They have left the retirees, the indigents, and the too-hip, from the class downtown, out of it. I imagine those others sitting in the amphitheater. Alone in the dark and the rain. I wonder: here or there?

"Interpretation?" says another. He is in the back, just beyond the spill of the work lights, where David went to stand. The lights are so bright, they press against my eyelids. It feels like a strobe, like heat and light and sinking darkness at the top of my head.

"No."

A door closes in the distance, and one of the standing ones, outside the circle, jogs across the warehouse. I hear his footfalls. The wind sucks at the building's walls. I'm the only one standing in the fucking spotlight. It won't do any good to go anywhere now. I light a cigarette and wait.

The jogger comes back, and a newcomer picks his way through the carpets—others move aside for him. The bottle comes his way.

"I'm sorry, Dr. Cade," he says. I've seen him before.

"You're late." It's a joke. Who cares? We're in a warehouse in the rain.

"I'm sorry," he says. "My other class got out late."

"Your other class?"

"Dr. Swanson's chemistry class." He digs in his duct-taped messenger bag. "She wrote a note for me."

"Did she?"

I look at Zoe. She's counting heads, writing down names.

Whatever.

"Meaning," I say, "is nothing so complicated. It is context."

They take notes furiously.

"Actions happen around us—to us. Even those you think you're controlling. They're . . ."

I can't remember.

"Sourced," Zoe says.

"They're sourced," I say, "by association." Saying it, trying to think it, is unpleasant. I wave dismissively, curling the air with cigarette smoke. I feel vertigo, like I'm afraid of my own height, standing on this concrete floor. It takes a moment to pass. Seems Cynthia hasn't taken this idea back yet, not fully. Repossession is with you everywhere.

They sit and wait.

"Probability . . . *sources* action," I say, through clenched teeth, "and it occurs some *place*, sometime. If someone smiles at you on the street, it means what it means. If someone smiles at you as you stand before a firing squad, it means something else. Context. The action that occurs within it is unimportant. The probabilities, the things you might, or will, or can do—that's what generates meaning out of context. What generates it out of you."

"Is this the same as the rhetorical triangle?" one says.

"Yes. Except, you can always change the context—you play at ethos by beating it to death with pathos and logos."

I pull my notes from my bag, trying not to vomit.

"Even when you're talking action, and not composition," I say.

I try to remember something else, but I don't. They will never get the conclusion to introductory composition and rhetoric. I feel like a fucking metaphor. Like college itself, the way it is now. I'm living proof of everything I'm trying to tell them. About how little selfhood or consciousness or being actually means. It's the best I can do, falling apart for them.

I'm doing this for them.

"Now," I say, "let's discuss research when you lack the resources to conduct it."

I gesture into the darkness for one of them to join me. She does. A small thing with hair longer than her arms. I hand her my notes, written on the map from my monitor shift, and point to the easel. She bends over to transcribe.

"These," I tell them, "are a handful of addresses, from neighborhoods across town. Work in groups. Find out what they *mean*. What contexts those spaces force upon us. You'll give argumentative presentations next week."

"In front of everyone?" one says.

That makes me smile. "You'll give them on street corners around town, and you'll grade each other."

They are quiet. The shadows, leaning in the back, exchange secrets.

"Time to try all this out," I say.

○

After class, Zoe leads me into the darkness. Most of the students disperse, deeper into the warehouse complex via its catacomb entryways. The ways into and out of this room are large enough to accommodate construction vehicles. The students pass through them several abreast. Like miners, looking for a way up, back to earth. Coal trains, from further into Appalachia, are the only ones that still pass along this line, but I have never heard of them stopping here. These warehouses were mostly for the textile industry, created on the backs of slave harvest in the south, so long ago.

The shadowy ones, the students who stood outside the light throughout class, make no show of leaving. They wander into other areas of this same chamber. Keeping watch. Something.

Zoe and I ascend a steel staircase. It climbs past the age-scummed windows near the ceiling. Outside, the rain still moves the light. The upper floors of this building don't have work lights, and all I can see are broken, dripping things. Once, people talked about revitalizing these places—taking them back from the artists and putting them to good use—because there was nothing else to talk about, standing in picket lines outside modern industrial parks and hospital entrances. The company officers and senior staff, whom they hated so much, had long since left them to stand alone on the pavement. To protest fate, even if no one was listening.

Some of the studios, in this district, still display the oversized American flags the artists found in their derelict buildings. Floor managers had once hung them between girders, so people behind machines could see what they were so proud of. The artists didn't have to do anything but frame them, and it became immediately controversial.

On the fourth floor, Zoe opens an office door—it has an unbreakable window. Filaments of diagonal wire in the glass, I understand, provide a view while repelling things. Like angry workers with steel implements.

She closes it behind me. The room resembles some sort of control room. Perhaps a switch tower for the rail lines. A series of brushed nickel work stations line the windowed wall. Their buttons are dark, their displays shattered. There are levers without handles. I can see the gantry tower below. The rain.

"Draw the shade, Dr. Cade."

The shade is just some form of oiled paper—she helps me uncoil it over all of the windows. When we've finished, I listen to her feet in the darkness. She turns on a floor lamp with a paper shade. It takes a moment for the low-wattage compact bulb to light up.

"Where are you getting the power?" I say.

She leans over the back of a sofa, stretching for another lamp. "There's a generator downstairs, in the old server room."

She rights herself on the couch. "We try not to use too much."

"I see."

Another couch sits on the far side of a large rug—something oriental. Threadbare arm chairs close the open sides between the couches—mismatched. There are piles of paper and envelopes on the glass coffee table, which is undersized for the arrangement. There are notes in red pen on the pages of an unfolded issue of *The*

Mountainist. Shirts and undergarments on wire hangers festoon a wall of steel pipes.

I'm still standing by the old work stations. "This is where you live?"

"It is now," she says.

"Hiding from the police?"

"You know about that?"

"You know they canceled my class. Looking for you."

"Why would I know that?"

That's funny. "Well. Do you have anything to drink?"

○

Sitting on the opposite couch, I can see her bed, now. It looks simple—a sunken mattress on a simple frame. In an old office behind her changing screen.

I watch her roll a joint on the table.

"Zoe, doesn't this strike you as a bit obvious?"

"What do you mean?"

"What *do* I mean." I'm still her teacher. "Tell me."

She looks flustered. She won't look at me. "I don't know."

"You're a smart girl," I say. "Figure it out."

She tucks a dread into her headband and fidgets with her joint. "Dr. Cade, I didn't—don't—mean—"

"Are you sure you've got it?"

She looks up now. "What?"

She's readied herself for the wrong conversation. Semantically. I remember that much. We're not talking about the same thing.

"Hiding here? In warehouses and galleries that are already known for artists and subversives?"

She looks away and exhales. "Oh."

I wait.

"Oh. Well." She gets up and waves a beckoning finger into her bedroom.

That stops me. But I am in control, here. I need to be in control.

I step carefully around the unmade bed. The piles of books. There is a small window, and she stands beside it, holding a pair of binoculars.

"Here," she hands them to me. "Look across, to the next building. Same floor."

All I can see is rain. A few windows and a roofline. I hear her strike a lighter beside my head. After a minute, an orange pinprick flares behind a dark window in the other building. It's gone.

"A watchman?" I say.

"Another resident," she says. "We have lots of lookouts."

I look at her.

"They have nothing better to do," she says. "We pay them in SHARES."

I wonder if she truly understands the concept of limited currency. I give her back the binoculars.

"That's good."

○

On the couch, she offers me the joint. Often as I've tried, I don't enjoy marijuana. And I don't want to smell like some other woman's pot when I get home. I have plenty of time. I only held class for about fifteen minutes.

I pour another glass of moonshine instead.

"I think it's time you answered some questions," I say. "You've taken over my class."

"I have questions, too," she says.

"I don't work for you," I say.

"Okay."

"You understand me?"

"I'm sorry. I didn't mean for it to happen. It wasn't my idea."

"Start talking."

She looks for something, over her shoulder. Looks back. "Do you mind if I chimp while we talk?"

"What?"

"There's a sim I need to try out. It's in progress."

"You keep chimping goggles here?"

She looks suddenly like a student. Someone young, toting computers and portable electronics from class to class across the lawns of a springtime campus. She trades messages with her friends and waits until her instructors aren't listening before she shares invitations to Friday-night parties. She is old enough to buy alcohol, so she can host them.

But campuses don't behave that way—not anymore. She looks older than she should be, at this age.

She owns chimping goggles.

I try to remember the timeline. Could she be the one from the bar? The network?

"Do you mind?" she says.

"No, go ahead."

"Will you join me?"

There's no reason to be a dick.

"Sure—if it makes you feel better."

◌

Zoe's goggles are smaller than the ones at the bar. Than Cynthia's. They look like old aviator sunglasses. There are tiny LEDs along the earpieces. The pair she's given me look normal. Like those at the bar. The tinted lenses make this dark room darker, which has an immediate effect.

The potential for action in context. Chimping is going to *mean* something right now.

"What's the sim?" I say.

"It's restricted."

If I could see her eyes behind the lenses, I'd know what her smirk means.

"But what is it?"

"It's just two people. You'll see."

I take the goggles off and turn them over in my hand, to be doing something. I can't tell which LEDs indicate what.

"Where did you get these?" I say.

She plugs my goggles into an adapter at the end of her line—the adapter into her mobile phone, which is barely the size of a credit card.

"They were a gift," she says. "Custom made."

A rich boyfriend, or her father. Someone.

I look at her phone. "Are we going to network this sim? Is that wise?"

She punches commands into her phone. "No, we're streaming it. The author won't let me download it."

"Won't the police be able to find you? Through your phone?"

"No."

I put the goggles back on. Lean back on the couch. It's old—the seams are worn and the batting is flattened. Like something from a community theater shop. Something donated, or stolen.

"Ready?" Zoe says.

I nod. She taps her phone a final time and grabs her joint from the coffee table. She leans back with her lighter for a long drag.

The room is as dark as it was before.

○

I don't feel anything. Zoe is humming softly—a steady tone, like something mechanical. Like Cynthia's sofa.

I pull the goggles off and check the LEDs along the earpiece. They're definitely on. The electrodes tug at the skin on my forehead

"Don't do that!" Zoe says.

I put the goggles back on. I can feel warmth now—it's radiating from the metal frames, pulsing in undetectable waves through my cheekbones, along my brow. Stimulating things near my brainstem and across the surfaces of my frontal lobes.

That's weird.

"Jesus. Are you okay?" she says.

"Yes."

"You shouldn't take the goggles off like that, not in the middle of a sim."

"Okay."

She touches my forehead with a dark finger, as if I am wounded. "You don't feel dizzy?"

"No."

"Sick?"

"No."

She drops her hand into her lap. "Okay. Tell me if you start to feel weird."

"I don't feel anything," I say. "At all. I was checking the goggles."

She uses the opportunity to lean in for a closer look. I can no longer tell if I sourced these actions on purpose. People are responsible for encounters of all kinds—conversational, martial, sexual. Someone is always to blame.

I'm not supposed to remember about behavioral subjectivity. And thinking about sourcing didn't nauseate me like it did downstairs. I don't understand.

"They're working," Zoe says. "It's working. You don't feel . . . *it*?"

She smells like tea. Like steeping leaves. Green things.

"No. What's it supposed to be?"

She tucks her feet under her legs and leans over the table. I see her dial up the intensity via the interface on her phone. I see the magenta polish on her toenails. It looks like blood in the goggled light.

She leans back. "That should do it."

Whatever.

"So, someone else is teaching, too," I say.

She stares at the ceiling, breathing heavily. It's getting to her—the new difficulty. "Yes."

"By coincidence?"

"No," she says, barely. "We reached out to some others. Trying to round things out."

I wait.

"We can't just study writing," she says. "You don't even grade our papers."

"I hear you have study groups for that now," I say.

She shrugs.

"Where did you find the others?"

It takes her a while. "A few of us knew some people."

"And you're paying them, too? With SHARES?"

"Yes."

"And you control who may attend class?"

She tucks her hands into her armpits. I can tell she is trying to get a grip. But I'm in control now. I still can't tell what this sim is supposed to be. My face feels warm, behind the goggles. Whatever it's trying to stimulate, in my brain, isn't there. Or it already is.

"We have to," she says.

"Why?"

"Not everyone can be trusted with the secret," she says.

"But you all can."

Her neck has become flushed. "What does it matter? The classes are still free, and everyone gets paid."

"The police won't like this," I say.

"They don't. We're hiding it."

"Which is why you use a fake name," I say.

She exhales, deflating. "Wouldn't you?"

"But they know the real one."

That makes her smile. "It's not fake—it's just my middle name."

"How many other instructors?" I say.

"Right now, ten. I don't know them all. Others do."

Now it smells like fruit in here. Like oranges and rose water. I look around for some candle or potpourri or whatever. I remember that people used to suffer something like this. These random smells, before we learned to condition it away. I wonder if this sim has conditioned it back in. Some side effect.

"You're starting a whole university," I say.

"Dr. Cade." She alters her position to recline against the armrest. This sofa is not as long as Cynthia's, but this is how we sit, there. "It's starting itself."

I drink my moonshine.

"You started it," she says.

I watch her curl and uncurl her toes. Her fists at her sides. "You're still not feeling it," she says.

I can't tell.

"Just remember," I say, "I don't work for you."

"We know," she says. "It's the other way around."

"What?"

"She feels . . . wonderful," she says.

"What?"

"This sim. Her index."

"Who is it?"

She rolls her head toward me and smiles. "Figure it out."

◌

"Do you all know what's happening to me?" I say.

"What's happening to you," she says.

"Repossession therapy. Renewal."

"We know. It's okay. It'll be okay."

○

The sweat on her arms, her thighs, is gold, lamped by the lights behind us. Beneath her black button-down, she was wearing a spaghetti-strapped tank top. Is wearing. A real-life tense shift. The shirt is pooled on the rug beneath the sofa, along with her jeans. She did not ask me how I felt about that. "It's the sim," she said.

I lean over and dial up the intensity. One last time.

She goes nearly limp.

"Zoe, what do the chimpanzees mean?"

She whispers, "Will you stay?"

"Here?"

"Here."

"Will you answer my question?"

"Will you stay?"

It's important to remember that I love my wife.

"You know you're a walking cliché," I say.

She just lies there and looks at me.

"The student, attracted to her instructor. She knows better."

"Yes," she says. "But only if this was my idea."

"What?"

"We're chimping, Dr. Cade."

○

"You think I'm responsible for everything I do," she says. She dials down the difficulty. "You taught us that we're not in control."

"That's not what I meant," I say.

"You don't get to pick and choose."

"Please. We all control our urges."

"Who's talking about urges?" she says.

When she pulls her goggles off, I do the same. She sits bent over, elbows on her knees.

"You didn't feel anything," she says. "The entire time."

"No."

She gathers her dreads in her fist behind her head and holds them there while she makes a note on her coffee table. She looks at me.

"You think I'm a stupid girl," she says.

"Zoe—no."

"Yes," she says. "You think I haven't thought any of this through."

I am no longer in control.

"Maybe I should just go," I say.

What was that sim? Who were we chimping?

She gets up and finds a band for her hair. The lamplight is sharp upon her legs. Crescents and lines of bright skin.

"I drove you here," she says. "Remember?"

Outside the rain thunders the walls.

"And anyway, you shouldn't just go because you don't like the conversation," she says. "Doesn't that mean I'm doing well?"

"I suppose so."

She lights a cigarette and leans against the busted control panels. "I said I have questions, too."

"What is it that you're supposed to be thinking through?"

She smokes. "You, class. Everything. What it's like living in a warehouse. Why I would do illegal things. People see a young woman, they try to tell her what to do." She gives me a look. "Even other women."

"Are you in some kind of trouble, Zoe?"

She folds her arms. Her cigarette smoke ropes past her temples. A taste of things to come—pale dreads, thin and smoky with age. Wasted youth. "What if I am, Dr. Cade? What will you do about it? Will you and your wife take care of me?"

I sit still. A teacher with a crazed student. An unwanted F. A dying grandmother. Problems with her degree plan.

"Me and my wife, Zoe?"

She stares at me across the industrial shadows. I wait her out.

"They told me therapy wouldn't make you stupid," she says. "Just forgetful."

"Who told you?"

"You know I cover for you," she says. "I fill in the gaps from my notes, when you forget your terms and principles."

"I know."

"I make sure the others are getting it. I don't even know what you expected us to get." She paces the control panel. "Which is why we filled in the gaps ourselves. It's how we got the other instructors to help. They liked the plan.

"You want to know what chimpanzee means," she says. "It doesn't mean anything, which is what has everybody so pissed off. It's just people with masks and spray paint. Leaving marks and causing trouble. It's an indulgence—a smokescreen. They just took the name from 'chimping' because they like the idea of being somebody else."

"Are you all chimpanzees?" I say. "Here?"

"Does that matter?" she says. "We're in a lot more trouble than they are, just running these classes."

"Then perhaps it's time we stop," I say.

"What's it like?" she says. "Falling apart like this. Doing collateral damage."

"That's just it," I say. "I don't know what's missing. That's how this works."

She looks down, young again. Sitting without pants in a cold warehouse. Looking thin and alone.

"We can't stop," she says. "People are counting on us."

○

Zoe navigates us out of the clustered warehouses. David stayed behind this time. He shook my hand as I left, in thanks or understanding. I'm not sure. He's a quiet kid.

I can see students through garage doors. Teachers with newsprint and easels of their own. I can see them calling on upraised hands. The rain is louder than the car.

We ride quietly up, out of the river bottom, along the rail bridge. Zoe drives past the bus stop and up my hill.

"You can just let me out here," I say.

She keeps driving and pulls up outside my house. "What does your wife think about all this?"

"What do you mean by 'this?'"

She turns to look at me, past me. I see her seeing the light in my home. Her face crawls with rainlight and unreadable emotion.

"Do you talk about it?" Zoe says.

I look at the house, too. At the water and the wind. I will be cold and uncomfortable when I step out of this car. "She doesn't want me to get into any trouble."

"Like I told you," she says. "People are counting on us."

She squeezes my hand. "You need to figure it out, Dr. Cade."

CHAPTER ELEVEN

W E'RE GOING TO FIGURE OUT WHAT MAKES THINGS beautiful, my professor said. He wasn't my director yet. I was still an undergraduate.

Things? I said.

Poetry, he said, literature. Took another drag from his cigarette, outside between buildings where the smoking ban couldn't see us. Political discourse, advertisements—anything, he said.

I was accepted to Northern, I said. For the creative writing program.

No, Ben. You're a good student, and there's more important work to do. We don't need more writing— we're going to figure out why there's any point in bothering in the first place. With anything.

How? I said.

He smiled. Sepia in the gleam of a sodium-vapor lamp. We needed to get back inside. The break was almost over. I think he created them for just this purpose. Having a cigarette. Night classes just ran too long. It was my final undergraduate semester, and this class was one last survey of everything worth learning, which you would only really do in-depth if you kept at it—in a graduate program. A self-perpetuating system of understanding. It would be really something at the top.

He tapped at his temple. Dropped an avuncular hand on my shoulder. We're going to *understand*.

○

I stop under the vestibule of an old bar, a place that served pizza and offered regulation-sized billiards tables upstairs. Dimitri and I used to come here, before it closed. We mostly talked about how frustrated we were with our jobs. His girlfriends. The price of beer. I always felt a little guilty, going out with Dimitri for a guys' evening. We'd always invite her, but Sireen usually wouldn't join us. She never has found any local girlfriends. Not since we left graduate school. Between me and her job, she's got it all covered.

I text her: Something is happening downtown.

I keep my phone in my hand. In my pocket, sometimes, I don't feel it vibrate. I don't use ringtones because they're intrusive. They bring your world into everyone's around you. It is rude and uninteresting.

Even the sidewalks are backed up. The avenues leading toward the old retail district are filled with unmoving cars. Most of their drivers have turned off their engines and are now sitting on hoods and kneeling on bumpers. Gathering against the problem, talking to see if anyone has information. Becoming a community by sharing their stillness. Suffering together, which is how they did it during the first depression—the Great Depression. Except now, the minute someone knows something, they will go back into their cars, to check their email and text their spouses.

Even the sidewalks are backed up. Pedestrians stand in slow-moving herds, approaching whatever-it-is that's blocking traffic. As if drawn by gravity or tropism.

What is it? Sireen messages.

Massive traffic jam. People are out of their cars.

Will you make your appointment?

Yeah.

It gets thicker the further I go. I can hear police sirens. People with upper-floor windows, along the avenue, stand and stare. Some gather on balconies to share what they can see. Like oracles outside of town, upon some classic hilltop—misshapen people and demigods and creatures with human heads. With all the answers. There is a price for the truth about all things. They already know what is going to happen when I get to it. They can see it from up there. Whatever it is. A singularity. A way to stop time and break a society.

The crowd is nearly impenetrable, upon the cusp, the event horizon. I can feel its stillness, the nothing stopping all these people. It radiates quietly, like a terrible accident or a giant meteorite. Something that must be stared at for a time, before we can figure out which experts should take custody and rope the area off. The cars here are stopped at odd angles. Like detritus, something littoral—they have pushed each other together as the tidal urge from the massed cars behind them rolled. Moved forward and back in tiny, immeasurable increments.

I can't get through the crowd, so I step onto the back bumper of a sedan that has become nearly perpendicular in its efforts to move away, around whatever is ahead of it. No one says anything as I crawl across the roof of the car.

There are hundreds of policemen encircling Sentinel Park—the streets around it. Their squad cars are nowhere in sight—no doubt they had to walk here, just like me. The only difference is that they carry guns.

There are people lying everywhere. In the streets, the crosswalks. They're piled half on top of each other along the sidewalks, draped across the chess tables above the park. People lie at angles upon, across, and along the amphitheater steps. There are no spaces between them. Each wears a pair of black shorts, or a black bikini. Some are in their underwear, which must have been the best they could do.

None of them move.

It's a protest, I text Sireen.

Around me, the crowd listens. What truth will come of this demonstration? Where were you when the people lay in the streets, confounding the police, causing problems?

I would guess, by their numbers, that this is most of the on-duty police force in town. Someone has gathered them all here, with these piles of useless, useless people. Doing nothing in the roadway.

What are they protesting?

One of the protesters is only a few feet away. Was he late, banished to the edges where it is less safe? Where he will be the first to feel teargas upon the soft tissues of his eyes, to feel billy clubs along his ribs, or even to simply be carried out of the way?

Or was he early? The first to lay himself down in this street. A way to stop the cars, the town, the police.

I force my way around staring people and kneel alongside him. He looks at me. He is young, but I do not recognize him.

He wears his protest upon his skin, like all the others. He is covered in text written with black permanent marker.

His forehead reads "Everything begins by making your audience pay attention." Zoe has learned to seize ethos—she has forced it out of her audience. This is physical, the science of changing motion with ideas. Applied rhetoric. They have no choice, these watchers. Me.

We're paying fucking attention.

I take a picture and send it to Sireen: Who knows?

I look, but there is not a chimpanzee logo in sight—simply smooth people in the urban day, unmoving. There are brilliant things between them.

I see Rosie leaning against a street lamp, staring. It would be difficult to reach him, and what would be the point? This is probably his lunch hour.

He isn't watching the demonstrators. He watches one of the clusters of police officers. He writes notes into a pad the size of his palm and whispers things to a young black man beside him.

Certainly, this would be the sort of thing he wants me to report.

I move away, along the edge of the crowd. On the other side, I can see people in a distribution line outside an old soda shop. The government didn't even have to buy the place—they seized it when the owners' back-taxes finally caught up. Unpaid. Criminal.

It is a good facility for distributing aid—there are several kiosks inside, behind the old fountain bar.

It makes sense.

The people in line move in small steps, a foot at a time. They don't watch the protest. They watch anything else, particularly the people leaving the facility, their arms full of brown relief bags. The police have cleared a small way in and out for them.

It's not a problem. There is another way to Cynthia's office.

○

Today, I am not permitted to lie on Cynthia's sofa. I must sit on it. She taps her pen against her computer pad as she stares at me. She wears trousers, hair in a bun.

"How is your house hunt?" she says.

I fold my hands into my lap. Whatever she is doing—however this is supposed to go down—today, I don't care.

"Fine. We were outbid on our first offer."

"Will you make another?"

"I'm here, aren't I?"

She reads something on her pad.

"We'll put the goggles on now," she says.

I know how to do it, so she stays seated. I pile the sanitary plastic wrappers from the adhesion pads on the cushion beside me. I pull the I.V. line out of its recessed coil in the armrest.

She looks up. "Not today."

I release it, and it snakes back into its coil, disturbing the pile of wrappers.

"Shall we begin?" I say.

She has a panel on her pad that interfaces with the sofa and the goggles. She punches at it with her pen, and the room darkens for me.

"I'm going to ask you some questions, Ben."

She's never made it this dark before.

"I understand."

I feel my phone vibrate in my pocket. A text message. I'm not sure I could even read it in this darkness.

"Can you tell me what 'affect' is?" she says.

"Emotion."

My head hurts. A sudden behind-the-eye pain. Some vessel gone awry.

"Wait," I say. "No. It is the *experience* of emotion."

"What is its significance?"

"I learned this as an undergraduate, you realize," I say.

"Answer the questions, please."

"Are we that far back? Already?" I feel like one of those people in the bread line. Welfared. I should have written something on my face, for Cynthia to see. *Affect is the experience of emotion.* I could lie in the street, outside her home.

"It is one of the three divisions of modern psychology," I say. "How far back have we gone?"

"Do you know the other two divisions?" she says.

"I'm sure I do."

"List them, please."

It's so dark. She is merely light. A being before me. The way and the truth. I feel hungry.

"I can't," I say.

"Try."

"You think I'm lying? Give me the answer. Isn't that your job?"

"Would you like a sedative?"

"No."

She brings something over to the couch, and the darkness smells like lilacs. I can see her because her blouse is white. A celestial body, dim and floating. Something to stare at behind tinted lenses, so you do not harm your retinas. When I was a child, I did this by punching holes in boxes and seeing the sun as a dot of white-hot cardboard.

Back in her chair, she brightens my view. I can see a pencil and a legal pad upon the cushion beside me.

"Please write down the other two divisions of modern psychology," she says.

I write them without thinking. *Cognitive. Conative.*

"Odd," I say. I no longer associate fully, consciously. I wonder if I will dream my education, when she is finished. If I will become something greater when unconsciously triggered. A still being, enlightened, counting breaths and shriving myself of psycho-social material baggage. Experiencing my old self as a series of confusing nightmares.

"Not all associative processes react at the same rate to this treatment," she says. "You still remember all three divisions."

"But you asked in context. Association," I say.

"Do you know what 'affective discharge' is?" she says.

I remember the term. I built my dissertation around it. The psychology of experimental fiction. The aesthetic implications of my director, my teacher, and what he did with affect, indexing madness. However it worked.

"Will you tell me?" I say.

She is quiet for a time.

"You don't want to know," she finally says.

"Why not?"

She is looking at her clipboard.

"You don't want to know how far back I've gone."

The door opens, and she stands without thinking. I remember that this is an act of one of those psychological divisions. It has important consequences.

"Excuse me," she says. "Get out!"

They push her deeper into the room, without contact, like some force of nature. She is repelled by a six-foot abyss between herself and the intruders. When they get closer, I can see it is because they are holding guns. They wear plain T-shirts and jeans. Bandanas across their faces, and sunglasses. One of them backs her into a corner and presses the muzzle of his gun against her throat.

The other stops in front of me. I shield my eyes when I look up, as if I am staring into the sun.

"You shouldn't be here," he says.

"I have an appointment," I say.

He grabs the wires affixed to my head in one handful. They come away easily. He isn't pointing the gun at me. He reaches for my goggles.

"Ben! Shut your eyes!" Cynthia says.

I remember Zoe in the warehouse. Her reaction when I pulled off the goggles.

I close them, and the room is suddenly cold against my skin when he pulls the goggles from my face.

"Breathe slowly!" Cynthia says. Her gunman does something. "He can be seriously hurt," she says, more quietly.

"Give me your phone," the gunman says before me.

I pull it from my pocket and hold it into the darkness. An unlit torch. My only way back to the light. Useless.

"You didn't read this text message," he says.

"We were busy."

"You should have."

"Hurry up," the other says.

"Just breathe deeply," the gunman says before me. "Keep your eyes closed."

I am not panicking. I am hungry, and the room no longer smells like lilacs. It smells like air conditioning and floor cleaner.

The gunman pulls something out of the sofa's access panel. I feel the tug through the cushions.

"What are you doing?" Cynthia says. "You can't. Those are *people. He's* on there."

There is a snipping of wires and the aroma of burning plastic.

"Come over here," he says.

I choose to understand that he means someone other than me.

"Give me your phone," he says.

"Take his hand," he says.

Cynthia's fingers are cold in my palm.

"Please don't do this," she says.

"Lead him out," he says.

"Please."

"Do it."

I follow her out of the room, down the stairs. I can hear one of the men behind me. Cynthia's receptionist is crying behind her desk. I can tell—it is a small waiting area. People are doing things here, but not what they should be. I can feel them around me. Celestial bodies. I have learned to see in the dark.

○

Outside, in the alley behind the clinic, there are more people. Cynthia lets me open my eyes, and I see that they are young. Like my students. They watch us, unmasked, smoking cigarettes. They are crowding the ways in and out of the alley, but you wouldn't see them from the street. I do not see any more guns. In the distance, I can hear downtown. The protest has become loud, and the alleys thrum with the sound of it. It sounds like a far-off stadium. Like they're having a good old time.

Cynthia has her arm around her receptionist, who is young. Once, she might have worked this job while attending college. Now she works this job to work this job. Cynthia stares at me.

"What happened?" I say.

"That equipment is dangerous," she says. "What they took."

I don't say anything.

"Your indices are on one of those chips," she says. "Among other things."

I can only think to laugh, but I don't.

"Would you like me to walk you somewhere?" I say.

"It would be inappropriate."

"Where will you go?" I say.

"To the police station."

"The police are all downtown," I say. "Tied up. Can't you hear the noise?"

Now I understand. The protest bought time. No cops free to bother our intruders.

"Then we will go there," she says. "Are you well?"

"Yeah," I say. "I'm fine."

But I'm trembling.

We walk in different directions. At my end of the alley, someone hands me my phone. I take it without looking at him. The messages have all been deleted.

CHAPTER TWELVE

THIS TIME, WE TAKE DIMITRI WITH US. OUT OF TOWN. THEY are both on Fall Break, from the university, and Sireen would like some air. Dimitri wants to photograph the kudzu, which is everywhere outside of town. He is wearing khaki pants and hiking boots. A short-sleeved shirt with multiple pockets. A straw hat. He sits in the back seat with a leather-bound notepad in his lap. Sireen and I wear jeans and old sneakers.

"How's the house-hunt?" he says.

"Fine," Sireen says.

"Fine," I say.

The radio slips between stations. The mountains are breaking up the broadcast into its constituent parts. Hissing and squealing.

"You know, ten percent of that radio static is left over from the Big Bang," Sireen says.

I wait long enough after she's said this before I turn it off. It's just noise, after all. Salvage, from the universal wrack.

"Will you make another offer?" Dimitri says.

"Yes," I say. I look over at Sireen. "Sireen has found another one she likes. A craftsman overlooking the river bottom."

"Great," he says. "That's great."

I turn our sedan off the state highway and onto the short avenue that constitutes this little town's main street. The trailhead we're seeking is on the other side of town—just outside it. Along this avenue, all I see are crumbling bricks and wooden siding, which has gone gray for want of chemical treatment. Between storefronts, I see glimpses of the houses that line parallel avenues.

"There," Sireen says, and points.

I park before a small, free-standing shop. The sign on the latticed window says GENERAL STORE. I can see candles and birdfeeders inside.

Dimitri and Sireen walk ahead. Around the building, there is a derelict wagon house in an overgrown lot. The mountains are watercolor blue in the distance. The building has been entirely overgrown by kudzu—it climbs the utility poles at the edges of the lot and hangs in geometric shapes from the power lines. Sireen and Dimitri wade into the weeds, and he points his antique camera at things.

Behind us, on the other side of the avenue, retirees sit in kudzu-vine rocking chairs, which you can buy. Some of the residents are weaving vines, making things. There are others harvesting kudzu leaves from a cluster abutting a parking lot. There are restaurants here that serve them in salads or vegetarian quesadillas made with thin, American cheese.

A few years ago, this town was the subject of a federal investigation. The residents ran underground cock-fighting matches that offered cheaper buy-ins and greater returns than the casino in the Qualla Boundary. They were run by young white men with beards and dark glasses, and you could buy jars of cheap liquor from the runners who came down from the hills.

No one used to come, from our city. It wasn't safe, until the residents began opening antique shops and selling their kudzu handicrafts. One of Sireen's senior co-workers gave us a kudzu-vine basket last year. It was filled with pears from the trees on the back third of his four-acre hillside plot, where he also grows tomatoes and paints images of the city below. Our city.

He is on paid sabbatical this semester.

The retirees across the street watch Dimitri take photographs. They see Sireen's unbound hair in the clear day. Me.

They are paying attention. Which used to mean something, even to them.

✺

Sireen leans her head against my shoulder. We're taking a break from the trail. She has an arm around me, and I can hear her nails picking at the ironwood tree against my back.

"I have an idea for a grant," she says. "For the department."

This is one of her professional duties. Bringing in money so the university doesn't have to fund its own research.

"That's good."

Dimitri is ahead of us, off the trail. I can see him on his knees, before a tree-of-heaven. Its leaves have begun their autumnal change, which will soon sweep all of Appalachia. People will come from the north to take photographs of mountainsides like acrylic paintings.

He is bracing his camera upon a log he found in the earth.

"Let me ask you," Sireen says, "is there a precedent for older scholars being indexed?"

"It depends how old," I say. "There are a few, older than us, who came late to the program, so they only had their last few semesters indexed. They were a control group—in a weird way."

"Because they couldn't lose everything?" she says.

"Yep."

"I see."

"And they were insured. My director and his bunch got the government to underwrite rehabilitation, if the experiments failed."

"Did they?"

"A few, but they're on lifetime pensions now."

"They're still collecting?"

"Well, they were," I say. "Times were fine then."

I shift her off of my shoulder, to get a better look.

"Why?" I say.

Dimitri is on his back now, obscured by the grass, lifting his camera through the tree's lower branches.

Sireen tucks her hair behind her ears. She squints into the conversation. "What do you think it would take to get them—the older ones—to agree to the process?"

"I don't know. Money? The backing of some foundation? People are doing weird shit with indices these days. Making sims."

She was shocked when I told her about the raid on Cynthia's office. My indices. She stared, as if she didn't believe me. Nodded a few times. She took a few notes when the police came by for my statement.

She nods now. It is a performance. It is a nod that says, *I already know what comes next,* but it's better, sometimes, if we look like we don't.

"Why?" I say.

"I was thinking, if we could get older scholars—accomplished scholars—to agree to index and then to donate it, then other people could use it. Open source."

Dimitri has finished with the tree.

"How?" I say.

"To solve problems," she says. "Difficult ones."

"What?"

"With chimping goggles. Like those people, from that sim at the bar. They were real. We *thought* them—like them—during that sim."

It's an oversimplification, but I can feel that pressure behind my eyes. I can't remember how to tell her.

"So," I say.

She crosses her arms. "If you could *think* like some genius, who has a record of solving problems, then you could solve more."

"I guess you could."

She studies me, catches the liminal forest light, alive and dying, in her eyes. We haven't been out enough—as much as we used to. Her skin has paled.

"Could I talk to Cynthia about this?" she says. "Would you mind?"

"No," I say. "I don't mind."

Dimitri is beside us now. His camera hangs on a strap around his neck. He has a bottle of wine in a cylindrical satchel over his shoulder.

"May I come to one of your sessions?" she says. "To take notes for the proposal?"

I don't know how long it will take Cynthia to replace the equipment in the sofa. Repossession is federal, so, a while.

"May I come, too?" Dimitri says.

○

He hands me a plastic glass filled with wine. Sireen found a suitable clearing, and she has removed her shoes to practice yoga where she can't hear us. I can see her across the trail, all elbows and sunlight. She doesn't want any of Dimitri's wine.

"Why do you want to come to a session?" I say.

He braces himself against the loam with an elbow. "Why does Sireen?"

It's a pinot. My favorite. Usually, Dimitri doesn't care for them. I can see the mountains over the tree line behind Sireen's clearing. We're both watching her. I feel like I've done this before. With someone, sometime. Watching Sireen, keeping an eye out. Checking for weakness in the other man. I wonder sometimes.

The wine tastes cold. Like earth.

"She wants to bring in grant money," I say. "Something about chimping great minds."

"Good idea," he says.

She sinks her belly into the grass. A practice of non-being. Reduction. There is nothing before us but a clearing of wild grass and the idea that there may be a woman within it.

"Why do you?" I say.

"I'm doing a study."

I look at him. His cheekbones are pale. His skin is manicured, and he smells faintly of cedar and rose oil. Some cologne.

We're so close to the Qualla Boundary, I want to laugh at him. A brilliant doll, like some shamanic talisman, who doesn't belong. He lives only this one life, but they live two, divided by those mountains into American and not. "Native" is just an afterthought.

"About repossession?" I say.

He looks back. "Repossession. People like you."

"There's not a lot of sociology involved," I say.

"Sure there is."

That stops us. We drink. Sireen stretches toward something—air, tension?—above the grass. I would rather be in that field, but she dislikes it when I interrupt her.

"Sure," I say. "You can come, too."

He hands me a cigarette. "I need a case study. I've been taking notes."

"Of course you have."

Sireen is the first to stop. On the way back. Dimitri is telling me about the albums he's copied for me. Most of them came from his students. I wonder who makes music anymore.

There are two white men standing between us and the trailhead, blocking our path. They're wearing ball caps and jackets. I move in front of Sireen.

"Afternoon," the blond one says. He lifts a hand. I can't tell if he's waving or halting us.

I walk closer. Within ten feet. I can hear Dimitri, or Sireen, following me.

"Hello," I say.

"I'm Ronnie," he says, "and this is Ken."

"Hello," I say to Ken.

"You folks have a nice hike?"

Ken has a hunting knife on his belt. I can't see what's under Ronnie's hunting jacket.

I can feel the anger. Like that sim. It wants to reward me, but I have to earn it.

"Yeah. You two ought to head up," I say. "It's a nice day."

"We won't take but a minute," Ronnie says. I can't tell what Ken is looking at.

"What can we do for you?" I say.

"We just want to extend an invitation. We've got a little place, outside of town. A bit of a farm—we're looking for workers."

"Thanks," I say. "We're taken care of."

"Who are you folks?" he says, nodding past me.

I turn my head. Make a show of looking.

"I'm Ben," I say.

"Steve," says Dimitri.

Sireen tucks her hair behind her ears. "Tina."

Ronnie and Ken don't move.

"Well, maybe you two'd be interested?" Ronnie says. He's staring at Sireen. "Y'all are all good Americans, aren't you?"

How much of Dimitri's accent could he have heard in "*Steve*"?

"Of course," I say.

"*White* Americans?"

"Listen, friend," I say. "We need to get back. The kids are at home with a sitter."

"It's a safe place," Ronnie says. "There's shelter and plenty of food. Plenty of protection. Your kids would be great there."

The insides of my elbows are starting to ache. There's pressure behind my eyes.

"It's open to all of us," Ronnie says. "You just got to invest whatever you've got. What you can afford, and we'll look after you."

"The whole town's involved," Ken says.

"There's no welfare bastards out there," Ronnie says. "It's the way it's supposed to be."

"Thanks, but no," I say.

Ronnie holds up his hands. "Suit yourself. We didn't mean to go alarming you folks."

They don't move.

"Maybe you'd care to make a donation, for our efforts," Ronnie says. "Give a little to those as aren't *taken care of.*"

"We already put five dollars in the trail box," Sireen says. Dimitri did. He insisted.

"Well, that's for the trail, Tina," he says. "For good folks like you."

"We're looking for the farm," Ken says.

"We're not carrying any money," I say. "We're hiking."

"But you had money for the trail box? Gas for that sedan?"

Ronnie takes a few steps forward. Ken staggers himself a pace behind.

"Ben," Sireen says.

I hold up a hand to her. This is a different me. There's a reason.

"I told you 'no,'" I say.

"Now, Ben—"

It feels like the sim, when I bury my head in his midsection, like my reward for giving in, for being aggressive. Dominant. The sensation of his fingers tearing at my hair is like picking scabs. Relief. The rush of his air across my forehead, as the trail comes up behind his back. The breeze through the sweet gum trees. The handfuls of earth that I grind into his eyes. Dimitri hits Ken with the half-empty bottle of wine. It doesn't break.

I fill Ronnie's nose with the air that I scream. Creation. I am the darkness he cannot see, from which all important things come.

I am remaking him with God's earth, where it becomes red in the pockets of his bleeding face. I leave him choking and crawl towards Ken, where he has pinned Dimitri in the leaves. I am my own missing link, learning to walk again.

Ken gets his knife from its sheath, and Sireen's shadow comes between us.

"Stop," she says.

"What are you doing?" Ken says to her. Dimitri cuts a glance at me.

I look at Sireen. She is brandishing her phone. Its camera lens.

"Taking pictures," she says, "of you."

Ronnie coughs behind me. She moves the phone, and it clicks him, too.

"I can send these to Renewal," she says, "with our location, or we can be on our way."

Ken lets his head fall against the earth. "You're a fucking monitor."

"Throw your knife into the woods," she says.

He does.

"Yours, too."

Ronnie does.

These two, fishers of men.

○

This is my girlfriend, Sireen.

My director nudged her in the ribs when he shook her hand. It took a strange geometry to pull it off.

Do you want to hear a joke? he said. He gave me his tobacco-toothed grin, like we'd planned this.

Sireen tucked her hair behind her ears, and he was excited because she was already smiling. If he only knew. I don't remember when I gave her the pearl earrings she was wearing. It was to commemorate something. I wore my sport coat, which my parents bought for me as an undergrad. This was an important lecture. The speaker was from   .

There was a reception afterward, and we made fun of the wine and the other graduate students. Sireen drank four glasses.

Yes! Sireen said.

How do you find an old man in the dark?

How?

It's not hard!

She laughed so hard she planted her palms on his shoulders. As if it might have knocked her over, and he took hold of her thin wrists gracefully. A gentle catch the way he might have held a door for her or led her through a waltz.

Nice to meet you—I'm Sireen, she said. Ben says so much—

Ben knows more about   -   - than any of my other students. I'm so glad he brought you.

They looked at me.

Well, she said. I always wanted to know more about   and   -whateveryoucallits.

' ! he said. Right, Ben?

○

On the way back through town, there is still kudzu. Still handicraft furniture and rusted antiques. I can see now, between the buildings, that the houses on the adjacent avenues have all been boarded up. They work here, it seems, the old and the infirm, but they sleep where it's safe, at that farm. I wonder where the young are hiding. Watching. What would Zoe and her friends think about this?

It's a good idea.

"You shouldn't tell strangers your real name," Sireen says.

"I needed to," I say.

"I know," she says.

"The phone was a good bluff," I say.

"I know."

○

We dropped Dimitri off at our bar, down the street. He wanted to go inside, dirty, scratched, to grab a drink and write. He smirked at me as he got out of the car.

Sireen didn't say anything as we drove up the hill.

I stand in the shower. I feel hung over. Heavy. The water runs brown as it carries the earth out of my hair, out of the tiny hollows in the skin on my arms.

My arms. That used to amuse me. Owning arms.

The tub beneath me is white. The tiles at my shoulders, white. There is nothing of liminal sunlight and grunting men in the earth, here. There is nothing here but white light—a clean space at the center of my universe.

Sireen steps into the shower, and I surrender the water. She looks at me, a white washcloth in one of her fists.

I don't know what to say.

"I don't know," I say.

Beads of clean water gather along her dark hairline.

"I'm not stupid," she says.

"I don't think giving them money—"

"I said I'm not stupid."

She dabs at the lacerations on my forehead. Ronnie became desperate as I piled the earth into his eyes. Trying to make him see. His fingernails were long and hard.

I think about the shooting outside the grocery auction. About Sireen screaming my name. It is a new feature of our lives together, like catching episodes of our favorite shows, or discovering a new restaurant. We scream now.

"Dimitri's doing a study," I say. She takes my hand, to dig the earth from beneath my nails.

"I know."

"About me."

She smiles. "What else?"

There is nothing but vapor between us. Thin and hot and white in this clean light. I think about the trail. About the dark mountains, the beech trees and the staring hawks. About everything outside this house—our life together.

In the woods, her skin looked like it had grown pale, but here, she is darkness. An evening-toned woman, a thing made of ribs and exhalations. The water in her hair smells like clay, and my fingers leave shapes where I press them against her shoulders.

I've had it backwards. Outdoors, we are nothing but what we aren't here. It is better, inside. We can be all ages at once on the sofa, or in the kitchen, or standing in the shower. We can be each of those things, those moments, that made us—that I keep losing to Cynthia. Our history doesn't need me to give it meaning.

She finishes with the washcloth. "When is your next session with Cynthia?"

CHAPTER THIRTEEN

"215 Sandway, 4021 Old Brevard, and 100 North Main," the kid says, "are all empty homes. They were foreclosed upon between fourteen and three months ago."

One of my students is giving his presentation on the sidewalk outside my bar. Two of his classmates sit out of the way, on the bench that once marked a municipal bus stop. They are wearing sunglasses and holding folded sheets of paper in their laps. Grading their classmate, as I instructed.

Or so I assume.

He sees me, but he does not break his presentation.

"Each mortgage was held by a different company—two local, one national. The local companies moved forty percent slower through the foreclosure proceedings, allowing the residents—Mr. and Mrs. Hamilton and their two daughters, at Sandway, and Mr. Vaughn at Old Brevard—to occupy the residence for between sixty and ninety additional days."

There are holes in his information, but I couldn't get much more out of the records office myself, when I compiled the list.

Three or four passersby have stopped to listen. They look up at him, standing with his legs askew on the supports of an enameled bike rack. The people wear plain shirts and pants they've stitched themselves from swathes of discount fabric. At one time, these fabrics would have made window treatments or pillowcases. Now they are clothes.

Their low-top sneakers are clean against the pavement. Sharp and washed.

"At my best estimate, thirty-eight percent of the homes, apartments, condos, and townhomes in the city are vacant.

"And where are those people now?" he says.

The watching people smoke cigarettes. One scratches at the tattoos sleeving his arms.

"What should we do with what they've left behind?" the kid says. What, indeed.

He hops down and whispers to his classmates. They disappear at a jog down the hill, into my neighborhood. The bystanders walk away, un-entertained.

I turn to see: a police cruiser trolls slowly down the avenue. I step inside the bar.

○

I select PARANOIA from the goggles' menu. The caption claims that the sim offers varying levels of a sense of causality. Of meaning between disparate stimuli. Something to believe in.

I think only briefly about the SHAREs in my pocket. About spending them on something other than alcohol. I'm getting better at not thinking about it.

As soon as the paranoia sim begins, I get it. I realize how fortunate I am that the squad car drove down the street. Who knows what other sim I might have chosen instead, given even a slight delay in my decision-making process? Causation.

This is important.

She finds me within minutes. I can't help but wonder: the students outside *this* bar, the police car, Zoe's custom chimping goggles. Everything in its coincidental place. I feel like everyone's behind this but me.

She chirps right into my ear phones—in the middle of something. "—/(n - 1)]*$\Sigma\{[(x_i - x^-)/s_x]*[(y_i - y^-)/s_y]\}$," she says.

"The fuck is that?" I say.

"You took Statistics," she says. There is a golf game on one of the TVs behind the bar. I am impressed people still play golf. Who plays golf? What agreements, deals do they make on that grass? Military, financial. Legal.

I hate golf.

"That was a long time ago," I say. "And how do you know?"

"It's public record, Ben," she says. "What you studied. It belongs to the state. And anyway, that isn't important. You've got what it takes."

"What?"

A stack of file directories appears in my field of vision—ever so slightly transparent. The directories list disorders—cognitive, social, etc. I have accessed these before. Each time I load a simulation.

"What's this?" I say.

"I'm sending you a simulation," she says. "Sit tight."

Directories scroll away, their names so immediately vanished and replaced by the interface's animation that I cannot make them out.

She must be Zoe. It makes sense. She's been doing this all along. Gaining access to how I think. I should tear the goggles off.

"Sit tight," she says, blurring through directories.

They're getting smaller, deeper. They flash and reload new file names in an instant. In less time than it takes my eye to track them, so I am not sure it is happening.

But it is, I'm sure. There's a term for it.

"What is it?" I say.

"It's new. A private simulation."

"Zoe . . ." I don't know if I can revisit that type of sim, like in her warehouse. If I should.

"My name is not Zoe," she says.

But everything adds up. There are causal relations between what I've seen and what's going on here. She's lying.

"Whatever," I say.

The directories disappear. PARANOIA ceases.

"But you can call me whatever you want," she says.

Is this the right timeline? Who else could she be? Is she even really female?

"That's better," she says. "You should stay away from paranoia."

"Why?" I say. She must have loaded the sim, but it doesn't feel like anything. I don't feel anything.

"It's difficult to manage, and it's addictive."

"So what is this one?"

"Correlation r equals one divided by the number of observations in the sample minus one multiplied by the summation of the x value for observation counter variable minus the sample mean of the x value for observation divided by the sample standard deviation of the x value for observation multiplied by the y value for observation counter variable minus the sample mean of the y value for observation divided by the sample standard deviation of the y value for observation."

"The equation," I say.

"Same as before. Only now, you get it."

"You told me it's statistics."

"So you're semantically primed. Put it together."

She's speaking my language. Something. The idea is gone as soon as it arrives.

"My wife would know," I say.

"You want to call and ask her to do your homework?"

"Cute."

"How much does she know about all this?" she says.

"It's about correlation," I say.

"Yes."

Now I'm feeling it. "This sim isn't a disorder."

"No."

"What is it?"

"It's just a way to think. What else do you know about the equation?"

"It correlates coefficients," I say. "In statistical samples. Where did you get this sim?"

"Does it matter?"

"I haven't thought about this kind of thing in years. Not like this, anyway."

"But you get the general ideas," she says. "That's all that matters. The sim helps you put the pieces together. The associations aren't yours. It's in the code."

"Now what?" I say.

"Do the math," she says.

"Cute."

"Think about it. Samples. Correlations. Why would I apply this to you?"

She waits.

"What are your students up to?"

"Giving presentations," I say.

"All of them?"

The simulation thinks me: "Wait. I don't know."

I realize.

"I don't know them all."

It hadn't occurred to me that they might have branched out. That, statistically speaking, the likelihood of whatever they're doing, in circumstances they share with others of their own age and ability across the country, would be an isolated system.

Except, the whole thing, the network of them, would be.

The sim knows.

"An isolated system," I say. "Entropy. $S = -k \Sigma [P_i \log (P_i)]$."

"Entropy of what?" she says.

"Information."

"Meaning?"

"The ideas are breaking down. My ideas."

"But you knew this would happen," she says. "You knew you wouldn't be able to finish what you started. It's why you started it, isn't it?"

"I was honest," I say. "I told them it was an introductory course."

"Which means they can do whatever they want with the principles. They have to fill in the blanks somehow."

"It's not about writing," I say. "Anymore."

Neither am I.

"Everything means everything else, Ben. Academic disciplines don't determine interpretation. The students have applied your ideas to other things, and they don't know you didn't intend that."

That makes me think. Free SHARES, cigarettes.

"How do you know these things?" I say. "We shouldn't even be talking about this. I could be arrested."

"Is there anyone around you?" she says.

"No," I say.

"Then don't worry about it," she says. "We're networking through a private server."

"Okay."

"For a cognitive scientist, you don't know much about communication technology," she says.

"I wasn't a cognitive scientist," I say. "Not really. I just studied the ideas. It was more like philosophy."

"And what were you going to do with that?" she says.

"Understand things."

"Let me ask you," she says, "how do you feel about the therapy? What's it like?"

"You want to chat," I say. "Again."

"Do you mind?"

I think about our past. The simulations, the anger and the compulsion and the mysterious information. She is like a college girlfriend. Fucked up and beautiful. She keeps me company. Someone I can talk to, about what I haven't told Sireen.

"It's not painful," I say.

"Do you feel different?"

"You mean less educated," I say.

She doesn't say anything.

"Only sometimes. Now and then things come to me when I'm not thinking about them. Otherwise, I don't know what's missing."

"I get it," she says. "Things still make sense."

"Some things, I guess. Important things."

"You should probably cancel your classes," she says.

"Probably."

"But you won't."

"Probably not."

"Why?"

"People are counting on me," I say.

"For what?"

"I'm not sure."

"People drag each other down," she says, "when they begin to drown."

"Who's drowning?"

"If you can't tell me, then it isn't you, is it?"

"I suppose not."

"It's nice to talk, isn't it?"

○

There are more people than usual in line outside of Rosie's trailer. Or he's taking longer checking each in. I can't tell.

After the woman in front of me leaves the trailer, it is several minutes before Rosie turns on the red "next" light beside the door. The buzzer sounds, and the electronic lock snaps open.

Inside, Rosie sits with his feet up on his desk, reading something. A newspaper. Whatever.

"Name?" he says.

"Cade, sir."

He lowers the pages and looks at me. He has rearranged the photographs on his desk to make room for his feet. Against the wardrobe wall, there are only a few renewal suits still on hangers.

Rosie puts his feet down and reaches for his coffee, which he keeps on a mug-sized warmer that plugs into the wall behind him. "Let's see," he says, situating his keyboard. "Cade. Crew 15, beautification."

"Do I need any equipment?" I say.

"Nope," he says, leaning back. "It's all on campus, waiting for you."

Campus. I don't move. It makes him laugh.

"Relax, Cade. They probably won't recognize you. Central is a big campus, and I'm sure you'll be wearing a respirator or something. It's yard work, you know. Unless one of the wardens picks you for asbestos removal." He winks. "But I don't think they will."

He picks up his reading again.

"Sir," I say, "may I go with the crews to the rockslide instead?"

"No," he says, turning a page. "You need to do this."

"Sir, please." I don't belong on that campus. I don't belong where Sireen's co-workers can see me shoveling garden manure, or blowing leaves, or mucking out the gutters. I don't belong where my old students will be attending their junior and senior seminars, now, talking about the importance of social progress and education.

He holds up his reading. It's an issue of *The Mountainist*. He's always got them piled around his desk. "You read this, Cade?"

139

I turn around and look through the window. The line is even longer than before.

"I've seen it," I say.

"It's always good," he says. "This issue in particular—" he flips backward through the pages "—about that protest downtown. You see that?"

"I saw it," I say.

"Of course. You had therapy that day." He points at me, wags a finger. "Good with appointments.

"Anyway," he says, "you should read this. Thing's gone underground—hard to get a copy these days." He turns the page around and points at the article. "This one, she's good—I like her articles. Leah Johnson, Cade. She has a lot to say about a lot of things. Seems the government has finally decided to tax SHARES."

Zoe has no idea. If anyone can find her, it's Rosie, with his thousand, thousand eyes. With his cell phones and text messages and workers who owe him favors. Like me.

How long has she been writing? How many has he read?

"Yes, sir."

How many of my classes have his monitors seen? The students and connections there?

"You know where most of those protesters ended up?" Rosie asks. He picks up his mug, but he does not drink.

"No, sir."

He spreads his arms. "Here, working off their hours against the common good. Those that weren't arrested, anyway. They tell me all kinds of things, Cade. Crazy things."

"Yes, sir."

"Some of them will have to be tax-collectors," he says. "For those SHARES. You know SHARES, don't you Cade?"

"Yes, sir," I say.

"Damn shame," he says. "Renewal just always cuts against the grain. It changes people—makes them do what they don't want. Makes them want to change things."

I look at the floor.

"Don't you think?"

I nod.

"Just remember, Cade. It's better this way."

○

They've finished the new chemistry building on campus. When I left, before, it was still a series of scaffold walls, like some giant wire sculpture. The idea of a building. Something sarcastic for the new age. *Remember buildings? Here's one.*

Now, it's a hard-lined megalith. To construct it, the administration approved the demolition of a commuter parking lot. Which didn't matter—it was never as full as it had been designed to be. Not during my final days here. There are wall-spanning windows, and bright concrete pathways that wind around and between trees, shrubs, outlining any route but a direct one. There are benches in strategic places, where one can sit and ponder chemistry. Each carries a tiny plaque to identify which aging alumni couple donated it. There are fresh squares of sod along the walkways, to heal the scarification caused by laying new sewer lines and electrical boxes.

The university had approved, drawn up, and broken ground on the thing before the full force of the depression occurred. Most of the funds were already in place—the panel that secured the grants to cover the rest of the cost were given awards and merit raises. The building is several stories tall, and it generates 65% of its own electrical needs via a system of solar, wind, and bio-diesel-fueled generators.

Someone has already vandalized one of its cosmetic stucco columns. A tiny chimpanzee with his head in his hands, stenciled clean onto the thing. Our wardens tasked two older women with cleaning it off.

A few of the students on campus watch us work Renewal. They take notes, cross-legged on the grass, as their professor points out this and this and this Renewal worker. Each one's particular job today. The color of its skin and its likely socioeconomic status. The ages of the workers. The students sit, on safari, and they secretly hope I won't come any closer, while they watch. Human influence always affects animal behavior, which ruins the point of watching at all.

Other students don't care, and we stop our lawnmowers and leaf blowers and trimming shears when they pass us on the walkways. The wardens told us on the bus not to let them catch us looking at any of the students, so we avert our eyes. We look at things like the sun, or our feet, or the ultralight panels of glass on the sustainable chemistry building.

Now and then, we look at each other. At how familiar we've become. Rosie is not randomizing the crews the way he should, and we're learning to trust each other. We're learning what that look could mean, on the young black man's face, holding the trimming shears, the one I saw Rosie talking to at the protest. The one who was in the trailer with another worker once. We can see in his face what else he can do. He hides expressions between the branches of sweat on his face, and we're learning to read them. He can tell what I'm thinking between my eyes. We all can. But we keep quiet. We think about the wardens and their guns.

The chief warden didn't send me into the old chemistry building. They sent half our crew to a hazardous materials tent, outside the old building, where they were outfitted with additional clothing and equipment to protect them from the asbestos inside, which they would be stripping from walls and shoveling into wheelbarrows. They would glitter with the light, with airborne particles of fibrous rock, thinner than anything but light, or maybe cancer. Later on.

I wonder why they're renovating the old building. What they will do with it. What other sciences or arts one can purpose a chemistry building for. Its tubes and histories and safety records.

There are temporary doors into the building that support polyvinyl ventilation tubing. There are signs that warn the students and the faculty away. There is a sign that identifies the job as another successful and worthwhile use of the Homeland Renewal Project.

Dimitri walks out of the tent. He is wearing a hard hat and the sport coat that he thinks projects an image of authority to his students. Men in black suits follow him out. A trio of students struggle with tubes of paper and clipboards, behind them.

I am holding a handful of weeds, which I have extracted from this flowerbed. I'm not far. It makes sense that Dimitri sees me, which is all right. He knows, so it's all right. He waves, and the burdened students follow his attention across the lawn. The class of students, with their pointing zookeeper, watch us interact, as if we are lifting plumage or dancing or ramming our heads against each other to establish which of us is which of us.

I wave back.

"Cade," the nearest warden says. He swings his shotgun off his shoulder. "What'd I tell you?"

"I'm sorry, sir," I say.

"You keep your eyes on the fucking dirt."

The worker with the trimming shears doesn't watch the dirt. He watches the warden.

CHAPTER FOURTEEN

FROM THE DAY SIREEN BOUGHT THE HOUSE, IT TOOK LESS than a week to fully close the deal and transfer ownership. Every entity in the deal—from the bank that owned the foreclosure, to the attorneys who monitored the signing, to our real estate agent—was ready to go. They have arrangements, teams. There are incentives to buy. We didn't have to make a down payment. Sireen's credit was fine. Which is to say what used to be average, which put her in the top two percent of eligible buyers. The realtor's office even paid for the crew to move our things into the new house—they'll arrive at our old place tomorrow morning.

The realtor left us a fruit basket and a bottle of wine on the kitchen counter. We didn't bring a corkscrew with us. We weren't expecting a round of drinks. We just wanted to walk around the place. Swing our arms and smile and listen to the hollowspace echo, now that it's ours. This is our chance to turn on all the lights and burn the evening glow of streetlamps and incidental shine from the windows. All of our curtains and drapes and bamboo privacy coils are still at the rental house, which leaves these windows as something obscene, without modesty or attire. This is our chance to turn our rooms into one-way mirrors, forcing people outside to watch us turn blind eyes to them all. We bought a house, and now they don't exist. We can't see them through the gleam of our own interior reflections. This house is now all houses—inside, with these lights, there is no outside world—nothing to see through the dark windows but reflected versions of what's in here, each containing thinner doors and coats of paint and pockets of wood-smelling air.

Let them see. For once, we have something they don't. For once, there was a point to all this. For once, I am not among the poor and disaffected. I am privileged and warm, staring at windowblack images of myself staring at myself. I exist endlessly here.

Not that it matters much. There aren't many of them to watch us—this nearly empty neighborhood.

There are three bedrooms. I find Sireen in the smallest one. When we imagined this, it would have been my study: a place for my books and vintage science fiction posters and stacks of student papers. The other would have been Sireen's study, and there would be the bedroom. Now, my study will be a nursery. I look at the ceiling fan and wonder if infants should have them in their rooms. The things I don't know.

When she sees me in the doorway behind her, Sireen turns around and runs past me. Without furniture in here, her laughing sounds haunted. Flat and damp. In the kitchen, she grabs the bottle of wine and smashes the neck against the sink. She squeals. We entertain ourselves by slopping wine into the glasses..

Outside our kitchen window, there is the river bottom, so dark-far below. There is the arts district, with its pinpricks of light traded by students with cigarette lighters in broken rooms, like fireflies. There is Zoe, beckoning to the others with the spark of her being.

But I can't see them, standing in the light like this, illuminating the hillside with the panes of my house, letting people in dark places know there is something better in the distance. Something safer than rocks or clouds or unstable terrain along the shore.

Sireen takes my chin between two fingers and turns my gaze from the window.

"Here we are," she says.

○

Cynthia's office calls.

"Mr. Cade?"

It's the receptionist.

"Yes."

"This is Dr. St. Claire's office. I'm calling because we haven't heard from you regarding the scheduling of your next appointment."

"I didn't think you'd be taking appointments. The equipment . . ."

"Dr. St. Claire isn't seeing patients in the office," she says. "The equipment has not yet been replaced. She's making house calls instead."

"All right," I say. "So is this just talk therapy?"

"No, Dr. St. Claire will be employing the use of her field kit. This is why we're behind schedule."

"A field kit?"

"Yes, it's for housebound or rural patients."

"I see."

"What time works best for you, and may I have your new address?"

○

Sireen and Dimitri have both prepared for this. They're excited. Sireen changed her jeans—which she wore all day while painting her study—for a pair of her professional slacks. She's wearing a sweater with a bundled collar that exposes one shoulder. She even took the time to hang our artwork in the front rooms of the house—where Cynthia will be able to see it. Dimitri has pressed his shirt, and he's wearing cologne. Just enough. He sits with me on the sofa while we wait. I mute the TV, but I leave the picture up—it's a documentary. About something. It doesn't matter. It's just something to look at. He volunteers his portable music player for the speaker dock beside the fireplace, and I let him play what he wants. It's something neo-folk. A song about being. Like the rest of them.

"Did I get you into trouble?" he says. "On campus?"

I don't look at him. I'm watching animated models of Pangaea on the television—how we might push our own continents back into its shape. Then how we might split them again, to make things right.

"It's all right," I say.

"I'm sorry," he says. "The chancellor told me I shouldn't call attention to you. Afterward. For your sake."

"It's all right."

A Renewal PSA commercial appears. It shows us smiling, and making the pledge of allegiance, and wearing red jumpsuits. We build roads. We feed the elderly. We keep an eye out for our internal enemies.

"What were you even doing there?" I say.

"Do you two want wine?" Sireen says from the dining room.

She's arranging hors d'oeuvres on the table. Olives and soft cheeses and tiny, gleaming knives.

"Please," Dimitri says.

"No."

I don't know if Cynthia is going to bring an I.V. line with her. Who knows how chemicals mix.

"Didn't Sireen tell you?" he says. He looks over his shoulder, as if identifying her for me.

"No."

"Tell him what?" she says, handing him a glass of wine. He brought two bottles of it. A housewarming gift.

"About the grant," Dimitri says. "I thought you'd told him."

She looks at me. "I told you about the grant."

"Yes," I say, "but what does that have to do with tearing asbestos out of an old building?"

Dimitri looks at her first. Then me. "That is the grant."

"Renovation?" I say.

"Yes."

"The school is renovating it to become a depot. For the perishables and other products that will come from SHARE taxation."

I watch him like a silent TV.

"It's a work-study," he says. "Community organizing and poverty studies will both route students through the program. Juniors and seniors, mostly."

"You've been working on this?" I say.

"I thought you knew."

"You know I use SHARES, right?"

He looks into his wine. "It wasn't my idea to tax them."

I think about it. I don't care.

"Don't worry about it." I slap him on the knee. "What do you think of the house?"

○

"You have a lovely home," Cynthia says. She shakes Sireen's hand. "Congratulations."

"Thank you," Sireen says. "We still haven't arranged everything. I'm sure it'll be months."

They trade smiles. Cynthia is dressed like Sireen. Professionally. Her shoulder bag is not unlike the one Sireen carries to campus.

"This is a colleague of Sireen's," I say, "Dimitri Petrić. He's in sociology, at Central."

Cynthia extends her hand, fingers together, cocked, like she's ready to pet a dog.

"So nice to meet you," Dimitri says.

"Likewise," Cynthia says.

"They wanted to observe a session," I say. "Sireen has some questions about indexing, if you can spare a minute."

"Of course," Cynthia says. "Support systems are important."

"Dimitri's doing a study," I say, "on the repossessed. On me."

"How interesting," Cynthia says.

Reflected in the taut lines of her professional hair, in its charcoal rays, the light in my house is not so bright. It is as dim upon her brow as it was in the windows. That first night, when I could still see what happens to the light when it fills the darkness.

"Wine?" Sireen says.

"Thank you."

○

Cynthia is not using an I.V. line tonight. She thinks a glass of wine is a fine idea, for me. So I agree.

Dimitri turned off the electronics when she asked. He and Sireen sit on chairs from our kitchen table, near the fireplace. Out of the way, with their legs crossed over their knees. Sireen's bracelet of imitation garnets rests against her wine glass, which she holds at a lazy angle against her crossed leg. The bracelet is too large for her wrist, which is fashionable. Dimitri keeps his shoulders back, his notepad upon his leg.

Cynthia's field kit is no larger than a portable computer. She arranges it on our coffee table and hands me a pair of chimping glasses, like Zoe's. Not goggles—these don't exclude as much stimuli as do the others in her clinic.

"They use less power," she says, watching me study them. "The equipment is not energy efficient."

I'm holding them by an earpiece. "What happened with the clinic? Did the police find anything?"

"Not regarding the thieves," she says, "but they face assault charges, if you'll press."

"Sure."

"Good. I have a form for you to sign."

I slide the glasses on. They feel light and hot and ineffective.

"There's one more thing, Ben, about the assault."

I look at her. An asshole wearing sunglasses in his own house. "Yes?"

"The technicians who appraised the damage to the terminal have discovered that it had been previously compromised by remote access. Several times."

"I'm sorry to hear that."

"Your data was among the information that was compromised, at successive stages during your therapy."

"Okay."

"There are reports of a rise in black market simulations," she says. "The Department of Health and Human Services regrets that your indices may have become a part of this trade."

I wonder if I could find someone chimping me. Talk to myself for a while about the good old days. I feel my molars coming together in the back of my mouth. I hold them in place. It takes a minute to get it together.

"Yes," I say. Carefully. "That's regrettable."

"I'll need you sign a form," she says.

"Of course."

"We'll begin, then," she says.

I stretch out on my sofa. I can feel the room behind the lenses, in the air that doesn't move against my skin—goggles usually close this off. These earphones are different. Cynthia's voice sounds tinny, cheap. The adhesive pads on my brow smell like talcum powder.

"Today, we'll do something a little different," she says.

She makes the room ever so red. I can see it in the refurbished coffers lining our ceiling. Sireen sits in the corner of my eye, adjusting the lay of her hands. I imagine her voice in the earphones, her fingers upon that computer pad, remaking my world in her image, just like Cynthia does.

An image of a frog appears in my field of vision.

"How does this make you feel?" Cynthia says.

"Fine."

She types a command into her computer. The pads warm against my head. The frog disappears and then returns. The exact same frog, the exact same position.

"And how about this?"

I think about someone, in some bar, saying my brilliant things. While I look at frogs. Am I even feeling this, or is Cynthia making me?

"Honestly," I say, "a little irritated. Why am I seeing this frog again?"

"That's okay," she says. "It's normal."

"What, irritation?"

"Seeing the same image."

I wonder how hallucinations work. How to perceive something that isn't there, bending light and air into the brain's best patterns.

"This is rehabilitation, Ben. You're at risk for neurological imbalance, now that we've made it this far. Just bear with me."

"Does that mean I'm going crazy?"

"It means you won't."

She shows me an image of her face.

"Who do you see?"

"You."

Then my face.

"Who?" she says.

"Me."

"Good."

I lean forward enough to sip my wine. I can't identify the grape, but it tastes faintly of mint. Nutmeg. It's nice. A pleasant evening with friends in the parlor, playing games with cognition.

"How do you feel?"

Who's next?

"Fine."

No, you try it.

"Very good," she says. "Now, something more difficult."

She removes the image of my face. Sireen leans forward, elbows on her knees. Dimitri is unmovable. There must be something about watching a friend, on a couch, losing his mind. It commands stance. Position. He can see best if he doesn't move, which is usually the body's way of trying to change the situation. The batting at a fly, the twirling of a lock of hair, the clenching of fists.

I can't tell what Cynthia's done, but I have clenched my fists.

"Are you a religious man, Ben?" she says.

"No."

"But you are familiar with the Bible."

"I studied it in graduate school. Narrative things in sacred texts."

"Yes," she says, "but you do not take personal meaning from such narratives?"

"No."

"Can you tell me how you're sure?"

She's fighting me with something. My teeth come back together.

"I just am."

"Did you ever find meaning in such narratives?"

My face is starting to sweat. My lower legs twitch.

"Remain seated, please," Cynthia says to Sireen, who is fidgeting.

"Ben," Cynthia says.

I would like to punch something with these fists. Myself, namely.

"What?" I say. It's difficult. My jaw adheres to my skull.

"Did you ever find meaning in such narratives?"

I can feel urine on my thigh.

"It'll be over soon," she says, "then you'll be safe."

"Yes," I say.

"What meaning did you find?"

The rest of my body begins to tremble. I want to run, to scream. I want to throw myself against the walls of my new house, to pass through them. To exist between chemically treated wooden studs and pillows of fiberglass insulation. I want to be something other than myself. Containing a version of myself that is not this version.

"God's voice, the formless waters," I say. "All of it."

"Why is that?"

"I—was—a—child."

"Do you wish now that you still believed?"

"N—o."

I shake I shake I shake I shake

I think I see Sireen turn away. I can't tell—her image is bobbing up and down too violently in my peripheral field. Dimitri looks like respiration. Something rising and falling without moving at all.

"Why, Ben?" Cynthia says. "You're almost finished. Just tell me why."

In an instant, I know what she wants me to say, how she wants me to psychologize my distant self. I know the lecture she wants to hear. This is me. All of me. Before I ever entered her office. Before I signed her affidavits and waivers and began showing up for Renewal shifts. She's given it back, and I'm thinking in grids, in longitudinal studies. I'm thinking about ontogenesis and affect and readiness potential. I'm thinking about semantic priming and the constructed nature of perception. I am scalar modality. I am a persistent self in Cynthia's therapeutic darkness.

I am.

○

My director was at our wedding. He danced with Sireen's mother and chatted with my friends from the program. He had made an art piece from one of the poems we were studying in the program—my favorite—and how we'd trussed it up with diagrams and charts to divine its beauty. Of all the salad bowls and blenders and sets of silverware we received, we cherished his gift most. It was a Saturday night, and Sireen and I would be back in our classes on Monday morning.

He danced with Sireen, too, and she smiled with him like a brilliant moon, full of contrast and hypnotic topography.

He brought her back to me, and he leaned into us. He smelled of old tobacco and sweet aftershave.

You're my best student, he said. And your bride is beautiful and brilliant and as unknowable as any line we parse or any paradigm we chart. Never bring yourself to her the way you do to the work. Cherish everything you can't know about her.

He looked at her. You do the same, he said.

She stopped smiling and nodded at him. I couldn't . . . , she said. Rolled her supernal eyes onto me. I remember, I could see the tea lights reflected in them. The chatter of our other guests clinked and giggled and coughed around us.

. . . because Ben doesn't make as much sense as math does, she said.

He smiled, and then he stepped away. He even had a hat to retrieve before leaving quietly through the double doors.

I didn't know what to say.

I will always take care of you, she said.

I know.

When she smiled this time, it was because she knew something I didn't.

No, she said. You don't.

○

I can't tell if the darkness is caused by the glasses or if Cynthia's equipment has agitated my occipital lobes, where all of this is taking place. She wants me to prove that I know what she's done. She's given everything back, for now, as a simulation from her machine, and this is the result—the collected nightmare of what she's repossessed. How she has reformed it, me, into something I can't physically handle. If I *were* capable of associating stimuli and information in the manners I used at the height of my education, if

I *were* capable—this would be the new me. Something condensed. A superconductor that can't handle itself—not without severe clinical intervention. This is how she has locked me into the walls of my mind.

This is what it is like, now, to think like me. It is called negative reinforcement, and we used to debate its effectiveness at training our young.

"I. Ca—n't." I say. "Too. Too. Too. Much."

"Ben?" Cynthia says. A voice in the night. She speaks from the surface, directly into my brain as I fall, fall into the wine-dark sea.

"It's me," I say. I don't know if she can hear me. I can't hear myself. "I get it. It's me. Before you."

"Come back," she says.

This is what I did, what I studied, what it was for—center stage. A heightened state of being, like agitated matter. Firing on all cylinders, the best and brightest I could possibly be. A state I could never achieve, not without Cynthia's chemical and behavioral accelerants. I never went through graduate school on purpose. I just didn't know what else to do. My friends stayed on, earned extra degrees. Sireen was there—she had a plan, and we're living it. I needed to be around her. It was all just an accident, understanding being. This is me understanding it, complicating it, realizing that it isn't anything at all. And now, how much worse I am for knowing.

I want her to take it away. I don't want this in my home, which is how we got it. Letting things go.

○

I'm no longer shaking, but I can't see yet. I'm still. A centered being. Like gravity on this couch.

Someone is running her fingers along my brow. I'm no longer wearing the glasses. I can feel all three of them, around me, like a medium at a séance. I am what they're here to see. What they wish to be near. I am the dark sun.

"Ben," Cynthia says, "what did you feel?"

"I don't remember," I say.

"But you remember feeling it?"

"Yes."

"What can you remember?" she says.

"Getting it all wrong," I say.

CHAPTER FIFTEEN

THE HANDWRITING IS MINE, SO I KNOW I HAD SOMETHING to say. I wrote it late, that night—after Sireen and I had sex in the empty house. Because I was still angry enough. Stealing my own knowledge before Cynthia did. It was something I wanted to teach—something they needed to know, then. But now, I'm not so sure. I can't know. I'm not even sure what all this is about.

But I have nothing left to teach, and I can't leave them without a conclusion. I must send them out to write and communicate in their unemployed worlds, their weary toil, with some reason to bother.

I must be a lesson in all this. A living example. They are doing important things, and someone must scream and march and call attention to himself. The center of gravity that keeps them together—a concept that exists, even though it physically doesn't. Someone must catch their attention while they build illegal universities and subversive economies. While they occupy derelict buildings and discuss philosophy in beautiful, useless circles. I smoke their cigarettes and spend their SHAREs and drink their moonshine. I give them lessons without context, so that they must make their own meanings. About what to do with a fading man. About what they think he's *really* telling them, even though I no longer know. I make them find help—how to fill in the gaps—and they find other teachers who do the same thing. All of us in motion. Things out of hand. Other important phrases.

Chimpanzee isn't real because they needed it not to be. They needed a diversion so they could safely stare at themselves in young, meditative ways—to watch the rest of the world in suspended wonder, trying to figure them out. The stencils and posters and subversive messages. The chimpanzee brand and its consequences. It makes people pay attention.

Chimpanzee doesn't *mean* anything, which is why it's so important. Like me.

○

This is the last time I will do this.

In the mailbox, I found a letter with an address for a private message board, online, with instructions not to enter the address into my personal computer. Which is Sireen's computer—the university issued it to her. The instructions stated that the password for the board was the most important of the three principles addressed early in the term.

The term.

I found enough change to buy a cup of coffee and ten minutes on a public computer at the franchised coffee shop two miles from my house.

I still remember: ETHOS.

There was only one message on the board:

NEXT CLASS. THREE MILE WALK. WEAR COMFORTABLE SHOES, DARK CLOTHES. A GUIDE WILL WAIT UNDER THE GANTRY TOWER OF THE CRISS BUILDING IN THE ARTS DISTRICT. NEXT TO THE TRAIN TRACKS. 7:00 PM.

I responded:

THIS IS THE LAST CLASS.

I called Dimitri and left him a message. An invitation to come along, for his study.

He texted me later. No thanks. Busy night.

I'm not inviting Sireen. This is bad enough.

○

This kid, my guide, leads me into the trees—state property along the railway, where it winds away from the city center. I can see headlights along the hillside, across the miles. They blink between the trees, climbing, climbing into the mountains. They look like magnesium flares.

This kid's got a flashlight with a red balloon stretched over the lens, so we can see without burning the darkness out of our eyes. We walk straight down the center of the tracks, where at least it's flat. The embankments abutting the tracks are nothing but loose gravel and twisted ankles.

I'm not sure if I recognize him. My memory is not what it used to be. A taste of things to come. He takes this seriously. He's got a walkie-talkie on his belt. It chirps at him every few minutes, and he holds it to his ear—looks into the dark as if orienting by analog waves. His comrades report distances and cardinal directions. It sounds like a moon landing. Something orchestral, polyphonic. The business of taking one's endeavor seriously.

We don't speak, but he looks at me sometimes.

✧

Once we're off the tracks, back into the trees, I can't see the city anymore. Even its overglow, which it bounces against the surrounding hills. It was brighter at night when Sireen and I first moved here.

There's a tent city in the trees. They use firelight. It comes at us, smokeless and inconstant. A glow like something else—some place with woodland creatures and supernatural people. They have a queen, but I can't remember her name. Some neat trick of Shakespeare's, but I'm no longer allowed to know. It would be stealing from the government—taking what's theirs, what they took back.

But at least there's that glow—it darkens tree trunks against itself, so that we might see them.

There are hundreds of tents, pitched in one long firebreak. There are clotheslines and windsocks and improvised metal stoves. There are yellow nylon ropes, hanging waist-high, tied to things in the trees on the other side of the break. Like traffic lanes or handrails. A way to know where you're going. To take a shit or have sex or disappear without getting lost. There are people in small groups, packing boxes and taping them shut. The tribe, on the move.

My guide leads me a hundred yards down the main avenue between the tents. We pass clusters of people in semi-circles, listening to lectures about chemistry, politics, military science. The instructors work with flashlights, which they aim at their newsprint-laden easels. Directing the eye to their hand-scrawled truths. Most of the instructors look older than I am.

Near the center of the camp, the brightest spot, the indigent's capital city, people stand in mobs. Families, students. Groups of young men wearing gang attire—their colors made uniformly brown by the firelight. There is a clear space with an untended easel. Students already sit in rows.

My guide leads me to a canvas tent—an antique with wooden poles and room to stand upright inside. It looks like some general's castoff, when he finished laying plans and making things true by discussing them with other men over inadequate maps.

Zoe is inside. She is sitting on a cot opposite another woman, on her own cot. There is a small, collapsible table at the far end bearing a battery-powered lantern.

"Hello, Dr. Cade," Zoe says.

I don't say anything. The other woman, who is older, excuses herself, and my guide follows her out.

"This is it," Zoe says, lifting her eyebrows and planting her palms on her knees. As if we are about to give an encore performance. Something that should make us nervous.

I take the other woman's place.

"I'm afraid so," I say.

She lowers her eyes.

"My therapist has taken what there is to take. It's over."

She rummages through a bag on her cot.

"Do you all live here now?" I say. "Are there that many?"

"No," she says. "We stay here sometimes, but they were here first. We bring them things, so they'll let us blend in."

She hands me a glasses case.

"Something for you," she says.

They're chimping glasses like hers.

"We can keep in touch," she says.

I put them on and stare through the rose-colored lenses.

"Have we been in touch?" I say.

She lowers her eyes, and her eyelashes are white, like spun glass in the lantern's cheap light.

"Have you figured everything out?" she says.

I could tell her that I figured out my own life. My new house and my civic duty. How light moves and touches the brain is all there's left to see of me.

"No."

But I'm not even sure that's it.

"It's probably better this way," she says.

○

Most of them come to listen to me. Those that can't sit, in one of those important rows, stand behind. People with nothing but these tents. Their children and past lives. The gangs come, too, and I see them clearing spaces so that others—more important, better-ranked—have a clear view.

I see the man with the angry eyes, from my Renewal crew—he who brandished those shears. Who held them still against the wardens and their guns. He waves—points me out.

I grab Zoe's arm. "There is a Renewal worker here."

"I know," she says. She doesn't struggle.

"Do you know how monitors work?" I say. "I do."

"They aren't monitors."

They. I let her go.

"They're invited—you don't have to worry."

"I'm not worried, Zoe—not about me."

"It wasn't my idea," she says.

"Let's get started."

○

"Those of you who have been in class, since the beginning, will remember the work we did in research, when one lacks resources."

They nod, in the rows.

"What was the point? Behind that information—those assignments?"

They've learned when I'm not actually asking questions.

I pull my lecture notes out of my back pocket—like a handbill I'd forgotten, right before doing laundry.

"There's something I wanted you to know," I say. "When I still knew."

I give them a good look. The faces in the light. Learning in the dark how to make truth. Training for the ages.

"Good luck," I say.

It takes me a minute to arrange my papers. I can't see well enough to read by the firelight, so my guide returns, and he brings his red light.

○

"The 'extended self' is the most fascinating," I read. "The most troubling. The ability to posit a future is what some claim separates the human mind from the animal's. But this isn't true. Animals are genetic futurists. Their very reflexes, like ours, choreograph futures. Muscle memory and spinal fluid are our best analogs for tomorrow. The mule deer stops, listens, perceiving threats without the inconvenience of a judgmental self-awareness. It twitches, jumps, listens—moves always away from those natural situations that posit a future wherein it ceases to exist. An alternate reality.

"Men with powerful rifles hunt mule deer for sport. Enforcing one reality over another, anticipating food and weekends in camouflage with other men around fraternal fires. Once, we did this with sharpened stones, and the fire had things to say in the voice of the dead deer.

"But the fear of nothingness is hardly selfhood. We know this. Nothingness is so often the goal. A quiet mind. A new pill—a better way of shutting up for a while. All things being equal. A temperature-neutral, safe place—homeostasis. This is what we seek.

"What separates us is that constant speculation about a reality other than this one. In the afternoon, we picture ourselves this evening. What will we eat? Do? Watch? And each possibility comes modeled—a partition in our own minds that creates, situates, animates the *us* in these not-yet-existent situations. Or in those that have already happened, placing ourselves in the past again. To do it right this time. Say this thing. Kiss that missed person.

"If we are modeling ourselves, states of being based on now, where do the imaginary 'we' exist? Where do our patterns of routinized logic, our entrained associations, our senses of being and fear exist? They can't exist in this mind, now, because we're talking about a different time, when none of this did, or will, exist. If we exist in these non-realities, anticipating predators and basing the non-existent future on the never-experienced past, are we us? We are another step away from non-being.

"We are all these empty houses—the ones you're studying. We are the homes that existed for other people, even though we cannot prove that. We cannot point to those lives except by referencing artifacts that only exist now. We are extending selfhood from 'here' to 'there.' We are the wince when someone else stubs a toe because it is *our* toe, too. We experience this happening to us, in a different place than this one, at the same time. Parallel universes racing infinitely onward, tracking domestic pains and forgettable damage. We are not here, there, fucking that person, not this one. Consciousness doesn't work that way. It likes to change what's come before, to better appreciate this.

"Selfhood is just the brain behaving, like running is legs moving. It's important to remember that 'we' are not in charge. The mind is not aware of the brain's processes.

"There's no such thing as time. There is no such thing as your home, your marriage, your children. There are only these so-many empty houses.

"We occupy old homes, the dead shells of other owners—their dust and tub-scum and home-odors. Our quiet evenings, and coats of renovation paint, and stillness in the night are not the activities of homes. They are us hiding from the predators in the savannah grass. The twitches and sniffs and moments of fear. The instants when we cease to exist because that must be a genetic possibility. A physical one.

"Homes are extensions of self. Expansions of consciousness. Places that think and hurt and make noise. They do not exist as whole buildings because no one can keep an entire house in his or her mind at once. Only the rooms that immediately, in fragments, concern your fear of death exist. There are sciences that prove this.

"You can call this solipsism, if it makes you feel better.

"But some people sleep in houses. Eat there. Create new people. The entire Danse Macabre.

"The extended self is the most troubling, for it must exist somewhere, and the mind violates time as it sees fit. The extended self—the liberated, freely roaming—is what separates us. It fears a world without—sells itself what marketing experts would like to. It is what builds empires.

"Don't get excited. It isn't a 'soul.' It's an operating metaphor that the brain uses to model itself in an inherently psycho-social existence with others of our species. Conspecifics. This is the last theory I mastered before I wrote my dissertation and graduated. It won't be with me, now, when you hear it, because my repossession therapist works in reverse order. What I am doing is against the law.

"Empty houses are like idle hands. The tools of the devil. When I was a child, I would break into them with my friends. We would tear mantel pieces off brick-faced chimneys. We would empty leftover five-gallon buckets of sulfuric acid into pools and hot tubs. We would write obscenities with oven cleaner on carpeted floors. A chemical that would stay—much better than a charcoal stylus and a cave wall. We would burn things.

"When we were caught, we defended our empty houses, told lies about why we were in them, because they were ours. Make a boy responsible for a home, and he becomes a man. Joins the community of other homes. Sleeps, and eats, and posits himself harmlessly elsewhere. Extends himself on sofas and recliners. Knows what it is to exist, a figment of himself, under other circumstances. Better ones.

"Which is the point.

"Breaking into empty homes is not difficult. Especially with assistance.

"But remember, sometimes, a house is just a house. A yard to mow. You build shelves and small things in the garage."

When I look at them, I see it on their faces. Divers too long underwater. Parsing knowledge like nonsense. I take the flashlight from my guide, and I drop the lecture in the fire. I leave them watching it burn, looking for meaning in the movement of light.

CHAPTER SIXTEEN

NOTHING REALLY HAPPENS ON THE DAY FOLLOWING YOUR grand design. You simply rest, trying to remember what the big plan was in the first place.

I walked three miles through the dark last night, after I finished— back across the rail bridge and up the hill to my beaming new home. After one mile, I was no longer interested in what I had done. I no longer cared what they made of my lecture, the class, themselves. Brilliance, and power, and meaningful actions are only around for as long as they're around.

Sireen was asleep on the sofa. She had our throw blanket twisted around her legs, her phone in a weak fist. I sat down beside her and watched the muted television, my legs full of those six dark miles. They felt light and infinite. As massless as flesh-pink nebulae, moving oxygen and heavy metals in meaningless patterns that, from far enough away, look like horse heads and crabs and cats' eyes. Toxically beautiful. Massive and throbbing, and heavier than anything I can imagine.

I sat and felt them expand. I became distant with each heartbeat.

This morning, I woke up after Sireen had left for work. My legs were sore. That was all. The day passed, and then there was another one.

○

The lenses of my chimping glasses are smoked pink, and without a simulation running, they make my living room look like salmon flesh. I watch the television through them, its red faces and brown-leafed trees—its skies like watercolor violet. Through these lenses. The public access channels were one of the first initiatives of the New Depression. The government bought a block of channels on credit, and it started using them for PSAs, educational programming—dramatic and arcane explanations for why nothing was working. We would watch spokespeople and university professors, in their offices, the backs of their heads bookshelved and out of focus, coaching us through the domestic effort, the unified ring, the very lump of contemporary being. They taught us how to say nothing in so many words, which was the best commentary we could use. The anthem for the New Depression.

It was considered an issue of public safety—making sure everyone had access to the government channels. The rolling losses of service began earlier this month, after we lost a telecommunications satellite. There was no going up for it, the dumb, dark thing. Space itself.

Today is only mine and Sireen's second scheduled loss of service. Two days, then it will be back. One has a civic duty, now, to alert one's neighbors in the event of a crisis, since we won't all be able to see the programs that will let us know.

The last stoppage was fascinating. Something to see. Objects in motion do not tend to stay in motion, not when the FCC pops your IP address into the blotter. The world went error-screen blue in one quick blink, and it looked afterward like the screen was expanding, to swallow the whole room. It's an illusion, caused by staring at the screen-motion for too long. One slides closer to the television, without moving at all. A traveler on one's own couch.

Today, the screen is violet when my service ceases. Because of these glasses. It comes for me: my house, expanding. We've done it, Sireen and I. The plan worked, and now, at the end of the world, I'm left with television light of the incorrect color, as if I magnetized it or dropped it, as if I forgot how to care for massless events.

But black is black, when I turn it off.

○

'

'   -

                    ,   .   ,
            ,   ,

            ,   ,   .   ,
                                    .
                , —   ,   .
            ,   "   "
                        -        .
                            ,   .

                            ,
                    '   "nothing," I said.
            ,   ,   .   .

                            ○

And another day.

The interface is different. The public goggles that I rent at the bar present the simulation titles in larger blocks of letters. They're easy to read, and there isn't much negative space surrounding the interface panes. The menus are tighter through these glasses. The resolution is higher, and there are expanses of semi-transparent, primary-colored panes at all edges of my vision. This software doesn't need as much space, not when you make all things sharper, and so the active panels bleed into the coolspace around the lenses, where my flesh is free to breathe.

There's a new simulation I haven't seen. Faith. It can't be that bad. I remember. They learned to electronically stimulate sensations of religious faith long before they began indexing anything. It's straightforward stuff. I roll the difficulty halfway up and broadcast my login. So she knows I'm here. A partner for a lonely man. Which was how God intended it to be. We aren't meant to be alone.

Faith comes on fast. I know what I'm here for. The genetic imperative. Seeking company and fellowship and a reason to fear darkness. It's best when you can fuck who you find, but sometimes it's all right to gather in groups just to make sure you've got the ideas down. The rules. It's how you make sure you're the chosen people.

She's as fast as the sim, my regular partner. Her network request is a digital hand-reach—the frontier of human contact. The network moves in mysterious ways, and she may not even be real. Pockets of software can gather in groups, too. There's a beginning for all things. A largeness beyond gathering data or ideas.

There's got to be a point to this. To her. The sim realizes this for me.

"Hello," I say.

"Ben," she says. That digital husk—translated sound. Technically, it's a voice without a throat to sound it. It's electronics. Without hollow flesh. I imagine it's how God would sound. "How are you feeling?"

"About what?" I say.

"Come on," she says. Irritated.

"I'm tired," I say. "That's about all."

"So you're finished with her?"

"Who?"

"The therapist."

I have Cynthia to thank for all this. The inner space. Absolution. It's how I can know there was a reason for it all. A greater plan for my being.

I could get used to faith.

"Yes, it's over. Unless something happens to me."

"So, how are you feeling?"

"Are you a real person?" I say.

"Why?"

"Well."

"You're chimping something."

"So are you."

"Do you want to meet me? To prove something to yourself?"

"I just need to know that you're real."

"You've already met me."

"So," I say, "that doesn't make you real. What am I supposed to do with you?"

She waits for a second. Trying to figure me out. Doing something.

"You know there's a grain shortage," she says. "You'll see it in a day or so."

"There won't be," I say. "I have reason to believe."

"The natives are getting restless," she says.

"Then at least they're accomplishing something."

"What is it you're after, Ben? What's the simulation?"

"Do you believe?" I say.

"Should I come over?" she says. "Are you ready for that?"

"I do," I say.

"Faith," she says.

"So you do?" I say.

"No. I can see your registry. You really should have learned how to lock down your information."

"I've got these new chimping glasses," I say. "Really something."

"This is pointless. Goodbye, Ben."

"I'll see you?" I say.

"Yes."

"Won't that be a thing."

"It already was."

✧

There are always days. There is at least this. They shed dust and light and evidence of their passing. Sireen comes in and out of the house, like tropism, following the sun so she knows when to do what, and what, and what.

I have never seen the cops who are standing on my porch. It makes sense—cops are always changing. Shuffling things up to keep the faces of administration young and sharp and disarming. Old cops make everyone uncomfortable, including themselves. They must heave and shift their bodies as they work. They adjust their flesh in piles beneath their uniforms when they get out of their cars, they move it around their weapons and utilities when they rise from their desks or sit down to lunch. There is no room left in their expressions for enforcing the law. They make it pointless, an obligation we must see to, like holiday dinners or trips to the nursing home.

It's better when they're new cops. Seeing the same one, more than once, when it isn't a coincidence, means that something in you has attracted the decay in them. You will rot together, whether you like it or not. Just like me. All these cops these days.

"Mr. Cade?" one says. He is wearing blue jeans and a windbreaker. His partner looks bored.

I've got the door in my palm. I made a great scooping motion of it when I opened it for him. He shows me his badge.

"I need to ask you a few questions."

◌

"Can you tell me where you were on Tuesday evening, between 8:00 and 10:00 PM?"

His partner orbits my sofas, my coffee table. He looks at the art Sireen hung. At the paint strokes on the wall, brushed or rolled—the tiny fibers and crusts of dried paint we left behind, shed by our implements and now painted into the plaster. He can smell us in here—perfume and floor cleaner and our particular fabric softener. He is an event, registering that yes—quite, yes!—we own this home. We've done it. Made it. And maybe, just maybe, my home wears the details of whatever they're here to question me about.

Tuesday. The day after my final lecture.

"Yes, sir," I say. "I was here with my wife. We ate dinner and watched re-runs."

He makes notes on his pad.

"We drank some wine."

The partner moves across the room. He looks through the curtains. Exists at the window for a moment.

"You recently completed repossession therapy. Is that correct, Mr. Cade?"

"Yes, sir."

"How are you feeling?"

"I'm tired a lot. That's about it."

He smiles. A young gesture, diving for teeth like pearls.

"I hear that's normal."

"Yes."

"Your repossession therapist was Dr. Cynthia St. Claire."

"Yes."

"And you were with her in the clinic when it was burglarized."

I wonder how necessary I am to this conversation. Does he worry that I have forgotten even myself? His partner is staring at me now, leaning against the entry to the hallway. Our bedroom is behind him. He fills the space. Establishing rank in my own home.

"Yes," I say. "How is the investigation going?"

"I'm afraid I can't comment on that."

"I see."

"I'm here about the attack on Dr. St. Claire."

"I'm sorry, what?"

"Dr. St. Claire was found on Tuesday evening, around 11:15 PM outside an old lunch counter at the intersection of Packard and Jarrell."

"What was she doing there?" I say.

He stares at me now, watching for that evening on my face, looking for my expression to tell him the story that I may not want to.

"We don't know," he finally says. He looks at his notes. "Her car was found a day later, two miles away, in the parking lot of a pharmacy near her home."

"Someone kidnapped her?" I say. "Dumped her in . . ." I think for a second "uptown?"

"I'm afraid that's not all, Mr. Cade," he says. "Dr. St. Claire was attacked . . . cerebrally. Her assailants forced equipment upon her and forcibly repossessed a great deal of her—" he struggles "—experiences in a short period of time."

I don't remember exactly. I know there's pacing involved. Cynthia didn't take everything from me all at once—it took months. The brain can only take so much excitation in a given period of time. It works like waves—come and go, come and go. A pool, a tide, a wave at a time.

"Wait," I say. "Why?"

"Our records show that you used chimpanzee iconography when advertising your outdoor class. Is this correct, Mr. Cade?"

I stare at my knees—only, I don't feel the staring. It feels as if it's doing it on its own. As if I am not in charge. I'm trying to figure this out. What would this do to Cynthia? To anyone?

I think about simulations. About what it must be like to chimp someone against their will. To be them, inside and out, as they were—in those final moments, before whoever took whatever.

I feel nauseated.

"Mr. Cade."

"Yes. I'm sorry. Yes."

"Have you been in contact with anyone from the chimpanzee movement?"

"No."

"Have you conducted class recently, Mr. Cade?"

I look at him.

"We're after Dr. St. Claire's assailants, Mr. Cade. Not you."

The partner takes a half step back. He's ever so slightly more now. A bit more of that hallway, those shadows. My life and room behind him. For a moment, I wonder if he's even real.

I touch my face to make sure. No, I'm not wearing the chimping glasses.

"No," I say. "Not since you canceled it."

He closes his pad. Stands up. "Thank you, Mr. Cade. May I contact you again? If I have more questions?"

"Sure. Yes."

I watch the partner watch me. A muted thing. Like staring at my turned-off television. He's simply there for me to know he's there.

"Wait," I say. "Is she all right?"

The cop scoops the door open for himself, following my example. It's the way to do it.

"Mr. Cade, Dr. St. Claire underwent the equivalent of six months of repossession therapy in, as best we can tell, a number of minutes. She spent two days in a coma as a result of the chemicals her assailants injected her with."

"She can't be a therapist anymore," I say.

"We expect this is tied to the same assailants who stole your indices," he says. "We'll be watching for the appearance of both of you on the black market. It's a rising trend. Stealing indices and simulating them around."

He extracts a business card from his windbreaker and writes on its reverse side. When he's finished, he brandishes it between us. "Dr. St. Claire is at County. Room 212."

His partner makes it out the door before he does. Like a shadow. Some extended thing. Being and not. I imagine he learned more than the talking cop did.

○

Dimitri and Sireen come with me. He had to cancel class to do so, but Cynthia is one of us now—one of me. The repossessed. She fits into the parameters of his study, so the least he can do is come along.

Sireen doesn't teach today. She gathered a small bouquet of flowers from the beds around our house. They were there when we moved in. Someone else once thought all of that space was lovely, too.

"Will she get it back?" Sireen says. In the back seat, Dimitri leans forward.

"Yes," I say. "I don't know. I suppose it depends."

Ahead, I see cars coming to a stop. There are police-lights spinning, blinking in primary colors on the sides of the road, just before the bridge. We're taking the back way to the hospital.

Sireen stares at her bouquet.

"Does the technology exist to put it back?" Dimitri says.

"It isn't gone," I say. "She was clear about that. It's been copied, essentially—I don't remember all of the trends, and habits, and things the technique indexes. But there's nothing to put back. It's still there. The problem is how severely she's been blocked from it."

I think. I still have the explanatory literature at home.

The traffic moves in slow fits. Like glacial ice. Our tires turn so little, with such force, that, eventually, we'll move the earth instead of ourselves. I can see people moving around, near the squad cars.

"She could be more blocked than you?" Dimitri says.

I think about it. "Mine is clinical. If I could pay it back, I could get it back, if it hadn't been too long—I'd just need a different kind of therapy, to overcome my reactions. Like you saw on the couch."

"And Cynthia?" he says.

"It wasn't clinical," I say. "They probably held her down and forced the kit on her. Who knows what they injected her with.

How much. Who knows why they wanted to block her out instead of simply making their own index."

"It sounds like assault," Dimitri says, "not theft."

"Who knows how much they went after. I doubt they were working from an audit record," I say.

There are Renewal workers ahead. Wardens with shotguns sitting on the hoods of their cars. The drivers in line ahead of us get in, get out of their cars.

"They might have scarred her. Like trauma. They've put her out of business for a while," I say.

"Maybe that's why," Sireen says.

"What?"

"To put her out of business. For a while."

Renewal workers approach the cars ahead of us in pairs. It's a checkpoint. Two come alongside my front bumper. The hood. My window and Sireen's. I see the pair at the car ahead. They gesture the driver out of the car.

I roll down my window.

He's bearded, this worker. A round midsection and crow's feet outside his eyes. A man who smiles and drinks beer in the evening, watching his shows.

"Step out of your car, sir," he says.

"What's this?"

"Please step out of the car."

I look across. The worker on Sireen's side is gesturing her out of the car as well. He points at Dimitri and waves at idle workers up ahead who are already finished. I watch across my hood as the driver in front of me leans against his car, hands forward.

"I'm a Renewal worker, too," I say.

He steps back so I can open the door.

"Then you can expect this," he says. "Probably your next shift."

They're frisking the man from the car ahead. Studying his license and asking questions. The Renewal worker has a small metal detector, and he wands it between the driver's legs, dowsing for secrets.

Across my hood, I see the other worker put his hands on Sireen's shoulders. He turns her around and she plants her palms on the car. Stares at me across the planes and paints and tiny hail dents of galvanized steel. It's supposed to just be the hood of a car. But not today.

We spread our legs, and a third worker settles Dimitri against the back of the car.

"Name?" the worker says.

"Benjamin Cade."

"Identification."

I reach back and extract my wallet; Sireen hands her purse to the worker behind her.

"What's your business today?"

She closes her eyes when his palms find her inner thighs. The lower inches beneath her waistband. I can feel the ridge of his index finger against my testicles. The heel of his palm against my spine.

"We're going to the hospital. Visiting."

He is not delicate as he drags the ridge of his smallest finger along the contours of Sireen's bra.

"Thank you for your assistance," he says. He steps back. "Enjoy your trip to the hospital."

They put us back in the car, and we sit quietly with our papers. They let five cars through the checkpoint at a time. We're number four.

Sireen reassembles her bouquet and stares at her hands.

○

"You're the first," the nurse says to us in the hallway. Her gait is evenly broken, the rolling strut of eight hours every day in ortho-pedic footwear. Standard issue, which the nurses pay for themselves.

She shows me her clipboard, so I'll care. There are no names listed under VISITOR IN/VISITOR OUT. I pull my lips against my teeth, tight together to make it clear I've gotten the message. This is how you do it.

"Is there family?" Sireen says.

"None that we've seen," the nurse says.

The door to her room looks heavy enough to repel germs and invaders. A cell and a fortress to partition degrees of healthy spaces down this hallway. Each room contains its own atmosphere. Its own pressures and smells and systems of discomfort. The doors bring division to overlapping categories. Pain, not. Healthy, not. Alive, not.

Cynthia lies in her bed. She stares at us, but she doesn't move.

Sireen puts her bouquet on a rolling table, which is askew, only somewhat aligned with Cynthia's shoulders, so that she might better eat from it, or drink from it, or reach its entertaining things.

"Just a minute, Ben," Sireen says. She goes after Cynthia's hair with her fingertips. She tends it, like a child Cynthia can't look after. It's oily, and the press of her skull against her hypo-allergenic pillowcase has flattened it in ways that look thin. Like chemo. She has a leg out from under her sheets, her gown in a pile over one hip. One does not wear underwear in a coma.

"Come on," I say.

Dimitri follows me out, taking notes, while Sireen makes her presentable. In the hallway, I stare at each thing for a few seconds in turn. I want to look like I'm comfortable here.

○

"How much do you remember?" I say.

Cynthia watches for a moment.

"Why you?" she says.

"We . . ." I look for help from Sireen. She's caught between a shrug and her uncomfortable smile. She has her arms crossed. Dimitri sits against the wall. He's discreet, with his notepad.

"I don't know," I say. "Why not?"

"You're my patient."

"Is there anything I can get you?" Sireen says. She sits on the bed, up against Cynthia's hips. She leans in that way some people can, occupying liminal space on sickbeds or sofa cushions. She compacts herself into someone who needs less room than normal, to simply sit and be present. If I were to try, it would be clear that I am uncomfortable, sit-leaning on something so small, putting up a larger performance.

Cynthia watches Sireen. "I don't know," she says.

"Did you speak to the police?" I say.

She changes targets. Rolls her eyes to my side of the bed. "Yes."

"So you know."

"Mostly."

"Will you go into rehab?" I say.

She looks at the ceiling. I am only just noticing that her eyes are green. Or I don't remember noticing. It could have been part of the repossession therapy process. Distance. Sterility. Keeping my therapist archetypal and unspecific. Something that makes sense in dreams.

"I am eligible for a federal pension," she says.

"If you go to rehab?" I say.

"If I don't."

Her lips are chapped. They look like stone. Like erosion.

"They would like me to make room for another," she says. "A recent graduate who hasn't worked the program yet."

Sireen looks at me across Cynthia's body. Across her cotton shroud, her vague topography.

"Will you?" I say.

"You shouldn't be here," she says.

"We just thought—"

"I'm not your friend, Ben. You are a damaged person. You require my attention to protect you from yourself."

"You're going to spend the rest of your life being you," I say, "you realize?"

She closes her eyes. Lifts herself into her own darkness. The room will be only red light through her eyelids.

"I remember it all, Ben," she says. "You asked."

"They're worried that we're for sale," I say. "Black market sims."

"You should go," she says.

"Who will I go to?" I say. "Your replacement?"

It makes her laugh. An expression of air—grit and humidity across her lips. "Jesus, Ben—you won't need any more sessions."

She finally touches Sireen's hand upon the sheets, but she looks at me.

"It isn't as arcane as you wish it was," she says.

"What isn't?" I say.

"Being you."

Dimitri stands up, against the wall. It catches Cynthia's attention, and they watch each other for a moment. Remembering other occasions, perhaps. An evening in my living room. Professional attire and cologne. This hospital room is the conclusion of anything they may have envisioned together. Consciously or not.

"Did you get everything?" Cynthia says to him.

He looks at me. I shrug. She sounds like no one impressive now. I sized her up, too. That first day in her office. Wondering about different lives and partners and intimate truths. It would always end with one of us undergoing medical treatment.

"Yes," he says.

"I hope it's enough," she says.

He stands at the foot of her bed. Wraps his fingers around her ankle for a squeeze. Something better than shaking hands, when one has a mechanical bed with plugs and outlets and intravenous lines in the way. There are indexing goggles hanging from the wall behind Cynthia's head, their wires spooled into a neat compartment.

"It won't be," he says.

"See," she says to me.

I'm not sure what she means, but I give her a good look. Like watching light in the darkness.

CHAPTER SEVENTEEN

SHE WAS RIGHT. THERE WILL BE A GRAIN SHORTAGE. THIS news program tells me so. Some enterprising journalist, at some dying news agency, leaked his under-normal-circumstances career-making exposé on some-or-other agricultural conglomerate's hush operation on the USDA recalls of its patented, genetically engineered wheat. This reporter was given a gag order by the Department of the Interior because his findings would likely cause a grain shortage, once the public learned about the recalls and demanded their enforcement, in turn costing the conglomerate-in-question millions in government contracts to produce the grain that produces the breads, cereals, and other sundry products that the unemployed are eligible to collect after registering at their local Renewal Welfare depots.

It is very informative. The journalist has been detained. People are angry at the Welfare Depots. Renewal workers have been given riot shields. The wardens fire a few shots.

I hope Sireen doesn't see this. She'll worry if Rosie sends me into crowd control.

I turn the television off. The world almost looks normal now, when I see things through my chimping glasses. Especially at night like this, when everything is already faintly red anyway. Orange. The sepia effects of artificial light.

Sireen is gone. She is holding office hours for the students in her night class.

I wake the glasses up with a stiff tap to the earpiece, and nets of public-access simulation menus come to light. There's a blinking one—a suddenly popular one—called FAMINE. I don't see the point of it, but the bandwidth numbers, in FAMINE's sub-menu, indicate that many do. They're chimping hunger by the thousands, teaching themselves what it's like to be hungry, desperate, then dead. They're watching the news.

I try it out.

A network request appears. It displaces my active menus. She always masks her account information, her IP address, which catches the glasses' attention. They dislike things without names.

I hear some white noise. Like static, if it could exist here. There's no room for universal noise in these digital networks. That leftover Big Bang buzz. As if it never happened.

I don't feel the sim yet. I wonder how much of it is about wondering when you'll feel it.

"Dr. Cade," someone says. Her voice isn't distorted. She sounds young.

No one I've heard before.

It gets me off the couch. I rest the fingertips of my left hand against one of the earpieces, as if I'm tuning in—holding onto a weak signal in the darkness.

"Who is this?" I say. My legs move me around my couch.

"There's going to be a party," she says.

Through the kitchen window, I can see downtown glow in the distance. Its still-lit grids. On important streets that still need light—that still deserve it.

"What?"

"We want you to come to the party."

"Who are you?"

"Students."

There have been reports of people in other cities getting into trouble. Students with underground classes of their own, marching and protesting and giving people food. They would like to be in charge, and they generate these ideas on couches in secret places. Drinking and smoking and having a good time in the New Depression.

"You shouldn't contact me," I say. "People are looking for you."

The sim makes me resent myself. I own a refrigerator, after all.

"It's safe," she says.

"The party?"

"Contacting you here."

I lean over the sink. With my forehead against the window glass, I can just see the old arts district across the river bottom. The service lights, affixed to its towers and gantry spans, don't work. I've never seen them on, as many times as I have looked, usually at night, passing through the kitchen and stopping for a glance as I move from one part of the house to another on important evening business. Usually, it's back to the living room with Sireen.

It sounds like patterns, that noise behind her voice. Something I should be smart enough to understand.

"What are you celebrating?" I say.

"Sometimes a party is just a party," she says.

"Is it?"

"Not this time."

"You can tell me where it is, when it is, then I'm going to close this connection," I say. "That's all you get."

It's an address. A time. A date.

Not long now.

I see pinpricks through these lenses. Orange dots in the dark warehouse windows. Like cigarette lighters. Like will-o-the-wisps. We used to put lights like these on our bridges and radio towers, to make sure helicopters and low-flying planes didn't smash into them. The idea began with lighthouses, and people tended them—kept them. We trusted them to protect sailors from our shoals and outcroppings—that sacred task, to simply throw light across the formless waters. Because it should be there.

The reality is that I'm too far away to see lights in those warehouse windows. But there they are.

○

She is excited, even if she doesn't want to be.

"A party?" Sireen says.

"Yes," I say. I have my phone in my hand. I'm calling Dimitri next.

"Sounds pretentious," she says.

I tug a pair of her jeans off the shelf in the closet. I'm smiling when I toss them at her on the bed.

It made her laugh.

We're going to be late, she said. I was making bad decisions. Trying to get her to wear a skirt. Again.

I dangled the tie over my whiskey.

"Look at you, professor," I say. "Too grown up to get drunk in some stranger's kitchen."

Don't you dare, she said. I love that one.

Wear the skirt, I said.

She complies. Legs out of her sweat pants.

"Can you blame me?" she says. "Who can we even drink with anymore. Grad students?"

"If you want to," I say.

This isn't a negotiation, she said. She downed her drink.

She throws her shirt at me. Trying to catch it makes me drop my phone. As if all tasks are difficult at this age.

It definitely was.

She's excited. She likes that I'm laughing in our bedroom. It's a good sign. We're just talking about a party, after all.

"Who's throwing it?" she says. She's taking her time with a new shirt. A different colored bra. She's pacing it—the encounter, the idea. Something other than our debts and this house. It's a reason to slow the flesh down. Keep things open a bit longer— that domestic way of doing normal things slowly in an erotic manner.

I stand like a moron in my closet, watching my wife. People pray and meditate and dance in circles for hours for this much suppression of thought. This simple frame of mind.

"Some scensters from around," I say. "There'll probably be music. Open invitation."

"Jesus. We'll be the oldest people there."

"Does that matter?"

"It's lame."

"We could use the air."

But she isn't serious. She's excited. She pushes me deeper into the closet and shuts me in. It's funny.

"Any requests?" she says.

She means her underwear. She hasn't asked in a while. But it's in the air again. Bodies and schedules on the mind, month by month.

I press my forehead against the closet door. "Surprise me."

Shadows move when she does, through the light underneath the door.

"You're right," she says. "We could use the air." I hear her feet on the bathroom tile.

I call Dimitri from in here, just to hear the closeness of my own voice in a small, dark space. I don't spend much time in closets. It seems about as unexpected as attending parties thrown by my old students. Somehow, I just want Sireen to see, now that it's over. That I'm done. Even if she won't realize it, I saw something through.

○

The neighborhood is as sparse as ours. At least one vacant house for every one occupied. FOR SALE signs like primary-colored trees stand in most of the lawns. A few houses are simply boarded up. Someone's financial embarrassment, sealed against anyone getting a clue or taking a look around.

There are more cars on the street than I'm used to seeing in neighborhoods like this, parked in parade-lines against the curbs. One of those suburban invasions. A neighbor with guests, helping himself to more street than he deserves.

"It's there," Sireen says, points. She's been counting house numbers.

The FOR SALE sign in the front yard says SOLD! A trio of yellow balloons climb thin ribbons into the neighborhood air.

"It's a housewarming party?" Sireen says. She looks at me. She's wearing dark eye makeup and bright earrings. She looks ready for this. Nothing like a math professor. Simply a woman who wants to look attractive. Sometimes, she's both, but not tonight.

In the back seat, Dimitri cranes his neck to see—surveying foreign lands, getting ready for the discomfort of sharing someone else's invitation. He has one hand idly on a case of beer. He insisted on paying.

"Don't worry," I say.

The students don't look too young, standing on the porch. There are three of them, holding cans of soda, and they wave as I drive by.

After I park the car, it takes several minutes to walk back to the house. Neighbors are behind their mini-blinds, their peepholes. Dimitri moves the beer from one arm to the other, and the heels of Sireen's boots make percussive sounds on the sidewalk. We try to be less foreign, try to avoid the public abrasion of being styled for a party but not yet at it.

One of the students comes to help Dimitri carry the beer. He's no more than a few years younger than I am. He wears plain clothes, and his beard is just long enough to need a trim. I don't recognize him.

"You all from the neighborhood?" he says.

We stop and stand with him.

"No," I say.

"Doesn't matter," he says. He gestures us inside, in case we didn't get the idea. "Everybody's inside."

The other two, on the porch, just smile. Young blonde women. The welcome wagon. They do a good job.

"This is weird," Sireen says into my ear. She has a grip on my elbow. A good one. I turn, but she's wearing her little smile.

"So what did you decide?" I say back.

"What?"

"Underwear."

She squeezes harder, shows me her teeth. It's an expression with more than one meaning.

There is only lawn furniture inside the house—folding chairs and tables with retractable legs. People carry drinks in plastic cups and mason jars. Cigarettes. Tank-top shoulders, and tattooed elbows, and leggings beneath short skirts. They lean against walls and create cross-legged circles on the carpet to share ashtrays and mobile phones, into which they jack several sets of chimping goggles—glasses, depending—through pocket-sized adapters. There are more people wearing chimping equipment than not, and the LEDs glow differently for each of them. Some are simply wearing a pair, no doubt, without chimping anything—some are fucked out on some poor bastard's index. Perhaps each other's.

I follow the front-door man through whitepaint hallways. He holds Dimitri's beer over his head as if carrying a torch. An oriflamme. Sireen has her hand on my belt now, behind me, which causes train motions between us, back and forth, as I start and stop through the crowd.

"What are they chimping?" I say to our guide. "The groups."

He glances sideways, bringing the caravan to a minute halt. "Home ownership," he says.

The fuck?

We move on.

David comes alongside, in the human shuffle, his hands full of cans of beer. I'm struck by how quiet everyone is. These are not loud people.

"Hi, Dr. Cade," he says, orbiting away, into the crowd.

I just smile.

Sireen makes a point of looking elsewhere.

Our leader changes directions. Dimitri isn't behind Sireen anymore. He blends in well. Is better at this than I am.

"Who bought the house?" I say to our guide.

"You're Dr. Cade?" he says.

"Yes."

"And you don't know?"

"No."

He walks us into the back yard and settles the beer on an overturned cardboard box. There are fewer people out here, gathered in small groups. Some are trying to light a trio of leaning tiki torches.

"Come on, man," he says. It's funny to him. "Nobody bought the house."

When he walks away, Sireen comes out from behind me. "What's going on? Are these your students?"

"I'm not sure. Some of them, I guess." I extract two beers from Dimitri's box. I hand her one with my best party motion.

Another student moves across the lawn. I recognize this one. He has the face of a waiter or a barista.

"Hi, Dr. Cade."

"Hi."

He smiles at Sireen. "Would you like cigarettes?"

She is stopped by the strangeness. Being offered plural. It cracks her suspicion, and she gives him an expression like seeing one's student in public—pretending against the oddness of being outside classroom authority. Of being equal and normal together. It forces difficult smiles.

"Sure, thank you," she says. Tosses her hair over her shoulder.

He hands her a repurposed pack. A full one.

"Good to see you again, Dr. Cade," he says.

I let him get away with it. *Dr.* Cade.

"Strange kid," Sireen says when he's gone.

"Come on, let's smoke."

We party like this. Avoiding everyone together. It's better than staying at home. We try to look busy with ourselves.

○

"I have to pee," Sireen says.

"Let's go."

Inside, finding a bathroom is not difficult. You can relate to all houses by their bathrooms. Their locations and specific designs against discomfort. The ways they mask the inconvenience of the entire domestic endeavor.

Sireen disappears inside one.

Dimitri is behind me again. "Come look at this," he says. He is carrying a can of beer that he did not bring to this party.

I follow him through the kitchen. A few people give us a look and then move away as we approach the door to the garage.

He turns on the light when we're inside.

It's empty except for the gas cans. Twenty of them. I can tell by tapping one with my foot that it is full. I wonder how long they've been collecting it. Through how many shortages?

"Some party," he says.

"What the hell?" I say.

"I think they're going to burn it."

They're up to something—the clandestineness and simplicity of a plan. Good plans aren't complicated or affected. The ones anyone ever really pulls off, anyway.

There are reasons to be here, for each of these students. There are reasons for them to have me here. They wanted me to see a bunch of gas cans in an empty garage, in a house none of them have actually bought. This is more than chimpanzees and stencils on city walls, or lectures in public parks. This is something they're doing—have probably been working toward for a while. A term project, under other circumstances.

I wonder if I assigned it.

"We probably ought to go," I say.

"You think?" Dimitri says. He sounds genuinely uncertain. In here, our voices echo. They sound metallic, as if we're speaking through chimping software.

The door opens behind us, and Zoe steps through. She has cut the dreadlocks out of her hair. It's short now, and it reveals the points and angles of her skull, how much forehead she's got to work with.

She wears dark makeup around her eyes, like Sireen.

"Hi," she says.

"Some party," I say.

With her hands in her pockets, she looks just like a girl, standing there. Nothing more.

She looks at Dimitri. "You found the gas."

"What's going on?" he says.

She looks at me. Raises an eyebrow.

"I have no idea," I say.

She stares at Dimitri. She's got something on him here. She doesn't look like someone trapped, caught. Like a girl with forced hands. I look at Dimitri, too—like the way people are attracted, in museums, to things others are already looking at.

"Leah is one of my students," he says.

Zoe does not look bothered by this revelation. She came out here to fuck him on this. She's making a move.

What can I say? *I* am her teacher. *We* have that dynamic. It has defined us—its borders and near-misses. What does it mean that she studies under him, too?

"Sociology?" I say.

"Poverty studies," she says.

I think about the warehouses, about those generators and the repurposed furniture and the unlikelihood of not being found there, when the cops were looking.

"It was a poverty simulation?" I say. "Are you fucking kidding me?"

I give Dimitri a look now. "You set it up. The arts district."

"It was part of the research for the grant," he says. "How to get at those SHARES."

I turn to Zoe. "What does that make you? An informant?"

She looks back. "A college student."

"You know the cops are after her," I say to Dimitri. "Which means you're fucking next."

"Leah?" he says. To her. He remembers, after, that I'm the one who told him. "No," he says to me, "I didn't know."

"They don't stay in your buildings anymore," I say. "They're on the lam." It makes me laugh.

He hasn't taken his eyes off her. "Sorry I didn't tell you," he says to me. "They were just doing double-duty—keeping an eye on you. A single-blind for my study. It wouldn't have worked if I did it myself."

"I don't really care, Dimitri."

"It's all there," he says. He gives me a hopeful look. "In the study—everything you did. It's preserved. All of it. You can have it all back."

"What? How?"

"They were just making copies, Dr. Cade," Zoe says.

"They?"

"Your wife, too."

"Copies of what?"

○

188

Sireen sees Zoe before we meet her in the hallway. She looks immediately at me. I don't introduce them when we come together in the kitchen. Sireen does not look angry or embarrassed. She looks happy to see Zoe. Happier than she was drinking beer on the back porch.

"You, too?" I say. "What were you doing?"

She ignores me and puts a hand on Zoe's shoulder. "Est-ce qu'il est prêt?" she says.

Zoe cuts a glance at me. "Ce n'est pas ici."

"You speak French?" I say to Zoe.

She blinks at me. Her smile looks like Sireen's. "Didn't you study any languages in college, Dr. Cade?"

"Leah's helping me with a project," Sireen says. She keeps her eyes on Zoe.

I can't tell what bothers me about this. I can't find the deception, from each of them. I'm not sure I didn't know.

"Wait," I say. "What kind of project?"

"Ça commence à être sérieux," Sireen tells Zoe.

For a minute, Zoe gives Sireen her full attention. She works this expression, this idea, like she's about to ask an embarrassing question.

"J'aurais peut-être besoin de l'aide," Zoe says. Quietly.

Sireen pulls her into an embrace. She quiets her. A hand on Zoe's shorn head. Small words in her earlobe.

I turn to Dimitri: "The fuck?"

He claps me on the shoulder. "I helped," he says. "I gave Sireen Leah's name. She's been helping."

"With what?"

"Keeping you here, man," he says. "Up among the living. We're bringing you back."

"You're not making any sense," I say.

Sireen releases Zoe. Sireen is taller, so she has to dip her chin to hold Zoe's gaze when she lifts her eyes, when she arches her brows to show Zoe whatever she's showing her. An expression of her own. A thing between women in a crowded party in a strange house beside a garage full of gasoline.

"Sure I am," he says.

"Leah's getting your indices back," Sireen tells me.

"From who?" I ask.

"Jesus, Ben," Sireen says. That little smile. "Don't be so obtuse."

"Did you break into the clinic?" I say to Zoe. "Jesus, did you all attack Cynthia?"

I turn to Sireen. "Why didn't you tell me this was going on?"

"Would that have been a good idea?" Sireen says. "Going to repossession therapy with the idea that we're getting it back?"

"We haven't done anything wrong," Zoe says.

"The fuck you haven't," I say.

They all stop. It comes together. All three of them. They're waiting. I've got to take it all in somehow. They watched me on my sofa. Pissing myself and convulsing, surrendering the last of myself to Cynthia's program. They told Zoe, and she knew, and the students took care of things. Me. Sireen let me fall apart on my own, so there would be a division, between what was happening to me and what it meant to still be a husband. So they wouldn't be the same. A man. A guy with a dick and a brilliant wife and self-absorption about both.

Sometimes, you aren't in charge.

I give up. I'm only fighting myself. They aren't even playing along.

"What am I going to do with my indices?" I say.

Sireen wraps her fingers around my wrist, in a fashion one uses in situations like these.

"How are your new glasses?" Zoe says.

"You guys want me to chimp myself."

They stare.

"It'll make me sick," I say. "You saw."

"All things in time," Sireen says.

I don't know about this.

I look at Zoe. "That garage is full of gasoline."

"Yes," she says. "And many others like it."

"If no one bought this house, why are you all here?"

"So the neighbors think it's ours," she says. "So they don't make a fuss."

"What about the real owners?" Dimitri says. He seems to surprise himself, not knowing what his students are doing.

"They won't check 'til Monday," she says.

"What will you do in the meantime?"
"We filled in our own gaps, Dr. Cade."

CHAPTER EIGHTEEN

SIREEN DOESN'T WAKE UP WHEN I GET OUT OF BED. HER hair is a fan across the expanse of her pillow. I spent most of the night unable to sleep, making shapes with that hair. Symbols. Arcane things that only mean anything on a pillow, in a bed.

I'm not going to report Zoe's gasoline. It's all I can do.

○

Sireen surprised me. She didn't wear any underwear, and as soon as she lipped this information into my ear, in the front yard at the party, while Zoe said goodbye to Dimitri, we started carrying that party thrum all the way home. I didn't think about my indices, or the gasoline in the garage, or conspirators and heroines and being everyone's biggest secret. Not then. Sireen held on every way she could, trying to make it happen. She has plans. We'll raise the kid speaking English and French. It'll be allowed to paint on the walls of its bedroom.

I think about it all now.

In the kitchen, I fill a tumbler at the sink. Through the window, it is as dark outside as in, so I stare into the river bottom I can't see. I wonder if Sireen thinks about math, sometimes, when she thinks about kids. About giving birth, breast-feeding, the dark worlds she contains. I can't understand the divisions. A professor, a wife, a mother. A modern twist on the maiden, the mother, the crone.

Something ancient and traditional. A quiet power, a series of roles that gets things done.

I thanked her, for getting everything back, right after I pulled away her jeans against the living room wall.

She gave me that grad school smile. That same expression, like she was up to something, walking down the wedding aisle. The look she sleeps in. The way she sees me beyond repossession and Renewal and my fascination with watching things fall apart. Like me.

"No problem," she said.

⚬

At first, they're nothing—my imagination come in from the woods, hiking along that river bottom. Dots or will-o'-the-wisps. Swamp gas. Tiny rednesses on the move.

But, eventually, they're as real as I am. Those people on the march, from the trees—red balloons stretched over their flashlights so they can see beyond their own glow. They hug the riverbank, in their long hundreds, carrying things.

I dump the water from my glass. There are a few fingers of bourbon left in our reserve bottle. The one we keep for Christmas or New Year's or emergencies. I pull it out of the cabinet, and it's slow in my glass.

I watch them come. They disappear into Zoe's old warehouses—one, two, a handful at a time, winking dark like pinpricks in windows. I watch them. In our bedroom, Sireen talks in her sleep.

⚬

The television is dead. I haven't been paying attention to the outage schedule. So I sit in silence at our table, drinking rebrewed coffee. I couldn't get back to sleep.

Nothing was moving in the river bottom when I looked again, earlier. The warehouses just look like themselves.

Sireen kisses my head when she comes in. That smile. It was a good night. She fills a tumbler at the sink, and I watch her stare through the window.

"Ben?"

"Yes?"

"Who are all those people?"

I guess they're up.

"What people?"

She moves to fill a mug. "The ones on the bridge."

I take a look, and there they are. People marching across the bridge that spans the river. Blocking traffic. Carrying signs.

"I don't know," I say. "The TV's out."

"Let me get my phone," she says. "Somebody's got to be talking about it."

○

"It's the grain shortage," she says. "They're protesting it."

"A protest?" I say.

She looks up from her phone. "I know."

"The police?"

She looks back down. The chatter from whatever feed she's streaming sounds like something bubbling. She has it turned down.

○

"Come see this," I say. Sireen is in the living room, listening to Dimitri's latest recommendation. Watching things on her phone.

She steps into the kitchen.

"Turn off the light," I say.

When she does, the fires are immediately visible through the window.

She joins me in front of it and wraps her hands around my elbow. We finished our dinner half an hour ago. I don't mind doing the dishes. It just takes a while.

The city glows, and I can hear sirens over Dimitri's music.

Sireen gets the bourbon out of the cabinet. She pours what's left into two tumblers. It's more than I'd usually pour at once.

So we stand there.

◌

"Riot police have been deployed," she says.

"I don't see anything about a riot," I say. I thumb my phone's browser to a different site.

"I think this is nation-wide," she says.

"Shit," I say.

"What?"

I turn my phone so she can see its face. "They're mobilizing Renewal for this. All of us."

She jumps when her phone rings. "Jesus."

It takes her a moment of staring at it. As if she's never used it as a phone before. "It's my mother."

She answers it.

"الو ماما."

My phone vibrates a text message onto the screen. It's not from a number I recognize.

ATTENTION, RENEWAL! ALL PERSONNEL PLEASE REPORT TO LOCAL DISPATCH. EMEGENCY DERELICTION IS A CLASS B MISDEMEANOR PUNISHABLE BY A FINE AND/OR 180 DAYS INCARCERATION WITH MANDATORY RENEWAL SERVICE EXTENSION. EFFICIENCY IS EVERY-ONE'S RESPONSIBILITY!

"ايه ماما، عارفة . عم بحضر."

◌

In the bedroom, I find my favorite Renewal-day shirt. It doesn't stick to the jumpsuit when I sweat. Most of my others do. The phone rings—the number is masked. It almost makes me laugh. Like I'm some kind of spy.

"Hello?"

"Cade."

"Rosie?"

"You got the summons?" he says. "You heard?"

"Yes, sir."

"Wear comfortable shoes."

"What? Why?"

He's quiet on the line. I hear a sound like wave motion, like digital noise. Something my new glasses do all the time. "Good shoes," he says. "Like, for jogging."

"Yes, sir."

○

All the smoke has curtained the town. I can see banks of it rising from behind one of the forested ridges. I remember the last time we had a wildfire. It took Renewal weeks to contain it. Dozens of them died, and there was an inquiry. Somebody resigned somewhere.

There are many more workers at the lot than normal. Rosie checks them in several at a time, and he deploys them, like squads. Riot shields, fire suits, construction vests. It is efficient. Workers gather and order themselves upon the asphalt. They shift positions, onto and off of the Renewal busses. They move in orderly fashion, seemingly nowhere, around the Renewal lot. The wardens stare at them like cattle. Something to keep an eye on. Movement is fine, as long as nobody gets spooked.

I ring the buzzer on Rosie's trailer. He ignores me. When the light finally indicates that I may enter, there is no one left in the lot. The wardens left the gates open. The wind across the pavement, between those gates and me, is dark and uncomfortable.

Inside, Rosie is cleaning his shotgun behind his desk. "Come in, Cade."

I let the door latch behind me, shutting out the smoke. In here, it smells faintly of vomit and body odor—the unpleasant accident of too many cleaning agents too often together. The place is spotless, in its surplus-furniture, refurbished-trailer kind of way. Things can be clean, but they will never be their original colors again. Their original brightnesses and edges.

Rosie watches me. The message lights on his telephone are blinking. Several of them. Things are happening, on that line, and he has quieted them for just this minute. There is a monitor's phone on his desk. He gestures at it with the muzzle of his shotgun. He has broken its back—hinged it across the spine, so that he may get his solvents into the barrel.

I take the phone.

He studies his gun. I know that he's paying full attention to me, but he would prefer that I think that he isn't. That he's thinking larger thoughts.

"Sir?" I say.

He snaps the barrel back into the stock. Making the point he was waiting for.

"You know I look out for you, Cade," he says.

Here we go. Every time, it's something else. He needs me to know he has things to say. He knows I know this, which is what thrills him. That I will listen. That I have to.

Even so, I'm not sure what he means. "Sir?"

"It's not just me," he says. "Lots of folks. You got people looking after you all over the place."

"Yes, sir," I say.

He puts the gun down. "Why do you think that is?"

"I don't know."

He gets up from behind the desk and puts a hand on my shoulder.

"You know, I don't even have to send you anyplace tonight," he says. "You could send in your monitor reports from right here."

He pulls a phone out of his pocket. It looks like a standard-issue monitor's phone, except this one has his name on it, not a serial number.

"I think—" he says. He pulls up the phone's messaging function "You've seen plenty. You just need a whole shift to type it all up."

"Sir?"

He plants his thumbs on the phone's keypad. Composes. When he sends his message, it takes only a second for my phone to vibrate. He looks at me.

The message reads, How is Central University connected to the activity in the arts district?

He doesn't move. He's just text on the other end of my phone now. I'm not even supposed to be in here, for this part of this particular conversation. It was supposed to happen somewhere else. Before.

I don't know what you're talking about, sir.

He reads it. Punches another message into the keypad.

"I'll tell you why it is," he says. "It's one of those things that happens. An accident. When other things come together."

What's your relationship to Leah Johnson?

We're still standing. Standing still. I can smell Rosie's aftershave. The lineament he applies to his joints. The detergent in his jacket. The paste on his discolored teeth.

I can feel my heartbeat getting serious. "I guess I'm just lucky, sir."

It makes him smile. "That's just it, Cade. Why are you lucky? Even after everything. After default. After repossession, you're still lucky. Things are still working out."

I lie: I don't understand the question, sir.

He reads it. Looks up again. "That isn't how it goes for most people. The ones I see here. Things go *wrong*, Cade. That's how we know who's ready to help. Who's got the misfortune it takes to change things." He's angry. "It's how *I* knew."

He sends another message, but he grabs my shoulder before I can read it. He gestures with his phone, like he might slap me with it or shove it between my ribs.

"You give me a reason, Cade," he says. "Send me anything that *compromises the effort*, I'll bring us all down. Her. Me. You."

"Sir?"

"You don't even get what's going on, Cade. You just wander your way through, and everything falls into place. It would make more sense if I just ruined everything."

He doesn't give me a chance to ask.

"Why?" he says. "Why, Rosie? What, Rosie? I don't understand, Rosie."

"I don't understand."

"If I ruined everything, at least that way you would understand what's happened to the rest of us. Caught up in your broken world."

He sits back down at his computer. "But I said I'd keep you safe, so here you are. I have to send you someplace tonight, or they'll catch it in the service audit. Monitor's as safe as you're going to get."

He looks up. "All alone. Late to the action."

"Where do you want me to monitor, sir?"

He lets go of me and turns around. "You'll figure it out."

I look at his last text message. It's a photo of me and Sireen at the party. She's talking to Zoe. Dimitri's back is turned. It looks like I'm staring directly at the camera lens, across the room.

"What the fuck is this?" I say.

He doesn't look at me. "That is collateral. If you compromise the effort, if she backs out, it all comes down. I'll keep these messages in my phone, and if I surrender it, they'll see how you didn't answer—what she's been up to."

"Who?"

"She said you'd cooperate," he says, "but I can't take that risk. You saw all those workers earlier . . ."

He gives me an eye. "All those soldiers."

"Soldiers?"

"Stop asking so many fucking questions, Cade."

He looks at the lights blinking on his phone. At his computer. When he looks at me again, there's pain on his face. There's a fucked marriage and an absent home and a dead father. There's joint custody of his kids, of his own life. A cot in a closet and a bottle of contraband liquor. A shotgun. There's everything. There it all is.

"Today's a big day," he says, "but it's just the beginning, and I've got to think about the long haul. People are counting on me. Here. Not least of all the federal government."

I understand that what's happening here should be clear. I should already understand what's happening. It isn't complicated. Rosie is not pushing me through labyrinths. Everyone understands everything, until they don't. I probably did understand, when I got started here.

"You've been safe," he says, "because that was her price. For this. People counted on you. *I* counted on you."

"Just tell me who you're talking about," I say.

"No," he says. "Not this time. Just *know* who."

"Zoe?"

He laughs. It's something he can't help. "You ever try to save an animal? When you were a kid? Like a baby bird or a little squirrel? Something that fell out of some innocent place?"

"Yes, sir," I say.

"Yeah," he says. "Me too. Got my smell all over it before my mama could teach me not to. God damn thing died anyway."

I watch him.

"Thing is, Cade," he says, "this all has to work. Now. Or it won't work anytime else."

He gets back up and stands in front of me. The whites of his eyes have gone soft yellow. There isn't much edge left in them. Probably hasn't been for a long time.

"You need to figure it out, Cade."

"Yes, sir."

○

I can hear their noise, deeper downtown. It sounds like the noise from Sireen's phone earlier—something bubbling. People are moving in important directions on all the sidewalks. Eyes down. Up. Jogging. Bubbling into their phones.

Dimitri is out of breath when he runs up to me, outside the Renewal Lot's fencing. He plants his hands on his knees and folds himself in half. I pat him on the shoulder. I'm not sure why.

"I thought—I would miss you," he says.

"What are you doing here?" I say.

When he looks up, his hair is tousled. Shirt's untucked, but the sleeves are rolled evenly. I can smell his cologne, even over the smoke.

"I heard about the summons," he says. "All of you."

I just look at him.

"I can't let you—alone," he says.

○

There are Renewal workers everywhere, I report to Rosie.

"Can you see anything?" I say to Dimitri. I've got a hold of his shoulder. The crowds seep like water, massaging things apart. Moving people in organic directions. I'm fighting the motion.

I know, Rosie messages.

All I can see is this smoky, Art Deco architecture. You can tell the smoke from the tear gas because one is darker than the other. It doesn't matter which.

○

The Renewal workers keep the people moving. The march is mechanical. The chants, the shouts. It's orchestral. The voice of God in the machine. The wardens watch their crews. Checking the herd.

Where did they all come from?

Recent enlistees, Rosie messages. Lot of them were yours. Demonstrators, too.

"Look," Dimitri shouts ahead of me. "They've set up checkpoints."

I look. Renewal workers pat and frisk. They issue civilians in safe directions.

Are you safe? Rosie messages.

○

Are you safe?

○

Cade?

○

The workers turn their riot shields on the police. The wardens. Shock and awe gone wrong. There is no reversing the insurgence. Wardens shout and gesture and shoot holes through people's chests. The shots are harder to hear than I would expect. They're less impressive than I imagine everyone wants them to be. And the workers kill them anyway, mostly with blunt-force trauma they deliver through the edges of their polyvinyl shields and the crush of their thousand, thousand fists.

The dead lie in piles with workers in blood-red vinyl. Like a protest. A taking of space to make us all pay attention. They've each got uniforms for this. Police, wardens, workers. It makes it easier to sort the corpses. Civilians shove and drag, pulling bodies into even lines along the sidewalk, as if they know a better way to arrange people on pavement.

The shields look reptilian in their scattering. Like scales. Slick and fractured. A sloughing.

Dimitri shouts something at me, but they're chanting now, and I can't hear him. He steers us through a different corridor of smoke, and we stop in some corner while a cluster of people thunder past. In a hurry. Places to be.

I'm safe. The citizens want food. They're shouting about grain. Workers have turned.

○

Stay safe, Cade. I said you'd be safe.

○

I stop Dimitri before he marches into a cluster of workers. They have a warden on his knees. One of them has stolen his shotgun. Has it at his face.

Where are you, Cade?

I can't tell. I shout into Dimitri's ear: "The fuck are we?"

He watches them. The warden cries.

Dimitri points, and I see the gazebo, just through a bank of haze. Sentinel Park.

○

They're shouting addresses. All those houses.

○

The fires make it downtown. The human crush is more than Dimitri and I can fight. We move away from each other, like continental drift or glacial crawl. Things we can't help. There are more shots. Chimpanzee masks. Renewal workers with bandanas around their mouths.

I'm leaving. Fires downtown now. Chimpanzee masks. I'm leaving.

You see now, Cade.

There aren't supposed to be chimpanzee masks. It wasn't a movement. Just people making noise. Distraction.

Distraction from what, Cade?

○

Cade?

○

All of it.

Ideas have consequences.

Like me.

Things work out, Cade.

Goodbye, Rosie.

○

I make it out because I am good at walking downtown. I know which blocks are the most vacant. I know whom to talk to. I know which times of day are safe for spending an hour in Sentinel Park, in the heart of downtown, doing nothing but being a guy with a coffee sitting in a park. It's my new skill set.

I can't see the river yet—our hillside. I try to text Dimitri, but I don't have his number memorized. It's in my phone. This one belongs to Renewal.

I run along the footbridge, alongside the pavement that spans the river. Cars have stopped in the road, caught by their own headlights, by what they're seeing in the darkness ahead. What they're hearing on those radios. Reading on those phones. My kids in the park, learning how to make people think. And Rosie's big deal. His workers, gone chimpanzee. Which means what it means. Now.

The city is on fire. There are pillars of it in all directions. People run around me, in both directions. No one is quite sure which way is best. Where they should be.

I pull my chimping glasses out of my pocket and jack them into my phone. I have to stop running to do this, and the crush of running strangers leans me against the rail. I can finally see the warehouses from here, my hillside, but that's it—not as close as it looks. I get the glasses on, the connection active in the phone. Now, when I look, I notice how many of these runners are wearing glasses of their own. I think about how many were wearing them downtown, chimping their way through whatever mindset it takes to revolt. To execute wardens and crush riot police with the mass of your own numbers. To own space by being. Like light.

Come on. Where are you?

She finds me.

"Ben," she says. She sounds nervous.

I'm running again. I choose a sim quickly. PANIC. Lowest difficulty setting.

"Where are you?" she says.

"I'm safe," I say. "That was Rosie's deal. He's in with the chimpanzees. All of Renewal is, it seems."

She is quiet, and the sounds of my slapping feet divide the seconds between us.

"Who did it?" I say. "Who brokered that deal?"

"They're burning houses," she says.

"Among other things," I say.

"You should go home. Your wife will need you."

"Zoe wasn't doing this on her own," I say. "Not *all this*."

I have to stop. I can't run and talk like this.

"There is a student in a chimpanzee mask on the local news," she says.

"Why?"

"He says they're burning to create meaningful space."

"What does that mean?"

"You tell me."

I can see ahead now. My field of vision is no longer shocked by each footfall, each panicked slap. I'm taking deep breaths, fighting this simulation. The idea is *not* to panic.

"He's asking the reporter what she thinks empty buildings mean," she says. "He keeps bringing up 'context.'"

I lean over. Plant my hands on my knees.

"The National Guard is mobilizing," she says. "The Marines."

The simulation moves shadows and bright corners through my field of vision. Things to make me jump.

"But chimpanzee isn't fucking real," I say. "It never was."

"Are you sure?" she says. "Your friend has found them."

"Who?"

"Dimitri. His text record indicates he found your students downtown. He's trying to find you."

"Jesus," I say.

The interface menus brighten in the lower range of my vision. There is a new simulation available. Its bandwidth is increasing so rapidly that the display isn't even numbers. It's just blurred symbols, like hieroglyphs, animated as they roll over and advance higher up whatever archaic scale. Whatever unknowable pace. It's popular.

REVOLUTION, it's called.

There are workers advancing behind me, from downtown. They collect people, running from their cars. Running downtown. Climbing up from the river bottom. Out of the woods. The workers put them in place and show them where to go. There will be no one to keep the peace, put out the fires, protect the common good. Without Renewal, nothing.

"Do you have the simulation they want?" I say. "The one that's . . . me?"

"Several people have that simulation," she says. "I'm one of them."

"How's it working out?" I say. I walk.

"Just fine," she says. "I know where you're going, what you'll do."

"How's that?" I say.

"I'm running your simulation, and I can already see myself doing things. Thinking ahead."

Downtown, where they don't want me—to protect me from myself—Dimitri and the students will bleed. Burn. Experience broken noses and suppressive fire. They will take rifle butts to the head. They will be detained and interrogated. Exposed to coercive electricity, harassment, molestation. They will be disappeared, dreaming of community gardens and underground currency. Of circular discussions and a real use for education. They will wait for me to finish what I started. To share the conclusion I was never going to be able to provide: the rifle butts and projectiles in the instants before they hit, when they merely share electrons with those parts of us at the outer reaches of physical space. The sense of being. The reality that vicious metal will soon occupy the brain-spaces where all of this has taken place. For each of us who played along. Did as they were told. Or forced. Or taught.

And across the river, Sireen waits in our house—an unsmoking safe place, bright over the water. The centrality of all things. My life and being. She waits to repair me. She will give me back what Cynthia stole. A bit at a time. The female of the species. And we will make children and mourn parents and fill that house with an entire life on high. Through our gleaming windows, this city will burn forever. Making room for something better.

People run. Chimping themselves through the revolution. Guiding the migration. Watching things burn. In fashions that do not induce panic, since we know how firefighters and riot police organize themselves—their prisoners and fires. We have plenty of their indices to chimp.

I think about the Qualla Boundary. About piled leaves and trail heads and the people who've intruded on mine and Sireen's time. What we were supposed to do and be. How it was all supposed to go. Why we wander woods and forests and antique sales in small towns. Why we feel the need to get out of town and ourselves. I think about Dimitri, wearing cologne to a riot. Ironed cuffs. I think of him losing that fight in the woods. Everything he did to help.

I remember something, and it makes my head hurt. I don't even notice this PANIC sim anymore. It just isn't inappropriate to the situation. The collective state of things. It fits right in.

"I offered once," she says "to tell you who I am."

"I know who you are," I say.

"Then what's it going to be?"

I know where I need to be. I start moving, in that direction I should. The light and color and shape of it, that direction, that future, that me that does not yet exist. Like the past I don't have, now.

Like a disguise. A chimpanzee. That either did or didn't mean anything at all.

I didn't even know. Or I knew.

I remember something, and it makes my head hurt. That we aren't in charge. That nothing is so complicated, so vast and important, as we would like it to be. Not once it's over, or repossessed, or burned to the ground.

"What's it going to be?"

I watch things burn. The world in Sireen's image—everything she did. For me. It's important to remember that I love my wife. Our lives together.

I know where I need to be.

I keep going. Running is just legs moving.

ACKNOWLEDGMENTS

"What reasonable man would like to be a city of demons,
 who behave as if they were at home, speak in many tongues,
 and who, not satisfied with stealing his lips or hand,
 work at changing his destiny for their convenience?"
 —Czeslaw Milosz, "Ars Poetica?"

By the time *Chimpanzee* finally let me go, its execution had spanned several chapters in my life—it followed me back and forth across the country, through several jobs, and into an entirely new sense of self. Which won't come as a surprise. Without help, though, it never would have found the page. My sincerest appreciation to my agent, Kris O'Higgins, and my editor, Mark Teppo. Endless thanks to my initial readers, who followed me all the way down the rabbit hole—Srđjan Smajić, Berrien Henderson, Roger Sneed, Trey Edgington, George Neal, Ashley Scott, and Cody Robinson. And for production assistance, translations, and expert opinions, I'm indebted to Aaron Leis, Laura Thomason, Daniel Boudreault, and, as ever, my wife, Rima Abunasser.

Darin holds a B.A., an M.A., and a Ph.D. in English Literature and Theory. He has taught courses on writing and literature at several universities and has served in a variety of editorial capacities at a number of independent presses and journals. He lives in Texas with his wife, where he dreams of empty places. *Chimpanzee* is his second novel.